Fireproof

Sasha Doyle

Contents

Prologue

The ground rumbles and the walls shake. I open my eyes to the usual darkness, I stare straight ahead as I get a sense of what's around me. I can hear my little sister's slow, steady breathing coming from the left, where I know her bed is placed. I wait a minute for the shake to come again. It doesn't.

I sigh, closing my eyes and rolling over on my side, placing my arm beneath my head. It was probably an accidental earthquake from one of the small children across the hall. Except it's the middle of the night and that doesn't make sense.

And then it comes again. This time it's harder. I snap my eyes back open. My sister's breathing has sped up. She's awake now too.

"What was that?" Her voice is hoarse; she's scared.

I sit up, glancing around the room even though I can't see anything in the pitch-black. "Azari." I whisper, "light a lantern."

She doesn't answer, but I can hear the shuffle of her bed quilt and the pattern of her feet across the stone. And then a small flame goes up inside a jar, matching the color of my sister's bright hair.

I can see now, the room in a dim glow where I can barely make out our bedchamber walls. Azari starts to walk back to her bed when the ground shakes. This time I hear a boom and I see my sister collapse to the ground just as the lantern falls. Glass shatters and the fire she lit is extinguished.

Now I'm beginning to panic. This is not normal; not some silly game the young Earths tend to play.

"Azari?" I ask, "Are you okay?"

"Ow." She answers. "What's happening? Why does the mountain keep shaking?"

I don't have an answer for her, but it turns out she doesn't need one. I hear the door burst open and I can just make out our mother's figure in the hall light. In her arms is our infant brother.

"Girls! Are you alright?"

"Yes, Mama." Azari answers for the both of us. "What's going on?" I can tell she's standing now. Good, she didn't get too hurt in her tumble.

Mother hesitates, I can tell she doesn't want to tell us. Or at least she doesn't want to tell Azari. "The mountain. . ." She starts. "I think we're being attacked."

I suck in a breath, throwing off my quilt and climbing out of bed. "Do we time to go to the Safe?"

The outline of Mother's head shakes. "Some are down there, but we won't make it. Our chambers are too high up."

"Erant 'iens mori!" Azari wailed. She was close to tears.

"Don't panic!" Mother told her, "It will only make things worse." She crosses the room and puts Baby Jupiter in my arms. She leans in close so

Azari doesn't hear. "Take your siblings and run. Don't look back. Keep them safe." She kisses my forehead. "Te amo."

Tears fill my eyes, threatening to spill over. "I love you too." I whisper before she leans down and says something in my sister's ear. And then she's gone, disappearing down the hallway. I know I'll never see her again.

Azari bursts into tears and Jupiter squirms in my grip. I shush both of them, tears running down my own cheeks. I'm only thirteen, but I have to take care of them.

"Aislee," Azari sniffles. "What do we do now?"

"We run." I tell her, remembering what Mother told me just moments before. "We don't look back, okay? We run and we wait until it's safe to come home."

She nods, taking my hand. I grip it back hard. And we run. Out the door, down the hallway in the opposite way Mother went. She went to fight, we're going to run.

The ground shakes again, the strongest hit yet. I stumble, but Azari falls again, pulling me down with her. I cradle my brother and turn so my back takes the blow. It hurts, but I'd rather hit the stone then drop Jupiter.

Loose stones crumble around us and I hear several lanterns breaking along our path. Our attackers are getting deeper with every hit. I scramble up, pulling my sister with me. Jupiter grips my tunic tight in his tiny fists, burying his face in my neck.

The corridor is dark, most of the light sources has broken. "Azari," I pant as we run. "Light our way."

I hear her rip off the tough fabric from the bottom of her tunic and suddenly I can see. Azari is holding a ball of fire in her hand, unfazed.

In times like these I wish I were a Fire, not a Water. It was a fifty-fifty chance though. Jupiter's type is unknown. He's too little. So far, his hair is brown, which indicates Earth. But that could change and based on genetics, it wouldn't make sense.

Another blow comes and the ground trembles. We don't fall this time; it wasn't as hard of a hit. Hopefully that means the warriors are fighting back stronger.

"My legs hurt!" Azari complains, but I know she's mostly just terrified.

"We're almost out." I tell her.

The long corridor finally ends, splitting three ways. Based on the tang in the air, and my memory, I know one leads down, one leads to the main cavern, and one leads towards the surface. Barely pausing, I take the surface tunnel.

More fallen stones are littered across the floor, and now I'm worried. What if too much has caved in we won't be able to go out? Now I wish I were Earth.

Sure enough, we come to a blockade of small boulders. I'm scanning the length of it when Azari lets go of my hand.

"I can fit here!" She calls. I run over to her, and despite the situation, Jupiter giggled as he bounces.

"Does it go all the way through?" She nods, her fiery hair waving. "Then go — here take Jupiter — I'll find another way out."

Her amber eyes are wide as I hand her our brother. "But, what if—"

I shake my head, blue curls hitting my face. "Run, and don't stop. When you reach the surface, head to the woods, out of the mountains. But stay away from Wolves." I am ninety-percent positive wolves are attacking.

The walls shake again and we duck away from more loose stones. Azari's eyes well up and she throws her arms around me. "What if you don't make it out?"

I hug her back tightly. "I promise I'll try, okay?" She nods against my chest and we both jump as another hit comes. "Take care of Jupiter if I don't make it." She nods again and pulls away. "Te amo." I tell her.

"Te quoque amo." She gives me a long, sad look before she turns and crawls through the tiny tunnel. We both know there's a high chance we'll never see each other again.

I let a tear trail down my cheek and I watch the light from her fire slowly fade as she gets farther away. As soon as she calls down the tunnel that she's on the other side, I turn and bolt down the corridor.

I know the tunnels as well as any girl my age. But I'm panicking, and I'm missing Azari's light. I told Mother I would protect them, and now they're alone. I need to get out, they need me.

The walls shudder and the stone beneath my feet split a little. I trip. And I fall. Hard. The wind's knocked out of me, and I gasp for breath as I try to scramble up. The ceiling caves and I'm buried beneath the rubble. And everything goes black.

Chapter One

An arrow wizzes by my head, hitting the tree next to my ear. A squeal comes from behind me, and little fingers grip my tunic tightly.

"Curre!"

I take off running, zigzagging through the woods. I can see the mountains in the distance. That's my goal. Get to the mountains, and home will find us.

Tree splinters fly as another arrow sticks in the bark. I zigzag some more, trying to avoid the darts flying at me from behind.

"Get her you fools!" A shout comes from the side.

I nearly trip. He's speaking English. I'm farther from home than I thought.

Jupiter and I have been out in the wilderness for four years, ever since the Caves were attacked. My sister, Aislee was supposed to be with us, but we haven't seen her since that day.

I slip on the leaves as my mind tries to fall into memory. Now is not the time.

An arrow hisses through the air and I jerk to the left. My brother screams and I can feel a stinging sensation in my right arm.

"Erant 'iens mori!" Jupiter shrieks.

I will my legs to go faster, and the stinging in my arm becomes a burn. I bite my tongue to stop from screaming. I glance back to see about twenty men gaining on us, all armed with bows and arrows. A few, I notice, have knives.

I'm not sure exactly who is chasing us. My best guess is Hunters. I don't think Wolves would have bows. They'd be in their shifter form. In spite of the situation, I'm still more afraid of Wolves than I am of Hunters.

I stumble as my mother's words come back to me.

"Azari, Aislee will take care of you. But if something happens, I need you to promise me something." I nod, taking in her words, well aware they might be the last ones I'll ever hear from her. "Don't forget who you are, or where you came from, okay? The wolf is your enemy, they can't be trusted. Stay away from the woods."

I've already broken part of that promise, as I'm running through a forest at this very moment. But I've been careful to stay away from Werewolves. Apparently we've been enemies for centuries. Wolves versus Dragons. Aislee used to tell me they were just jealous. They could shift, like us, but we had extra abilities.

Excruciating pain erupts in my calf. I cry out, falling forwards and letting go of Jupiter. "Salire!" I tell him.

I crumple to the ground and he leaps off my back, shifting mid-jump. I grimace, knowing how important it is to keep our abilities a secret. Jupiter is five, he doesn't understand. So I let him attack, my eyes becoming blurry.

I start to feel lightheaded, so I scan my body for injuries, starting with the obvious arrow lodged in my calf. I tug it out, yelping as I do so. I notice blood running down my right arm, but it isn't as bad as my leg.

Black dots dance at the edge of my vision and I fight it, keeping one eye on my brother.

Jupiter's dragon is a golden-blonde color. Chestnut brown spikes stick up along his spine, trailing all the way down to his tail. His eyes glow an electric yellow.

He opens his mouth, showing rows of tiny needle-sharp teeth. The Hunters huddle in front of him, a few trying to sneak past and get to me. Jupiter lets out a roar, stopping them each time, defending me. Pride for my baby brother rushes through me, but I'm close to passing out.

Hold on. My dragon, Kenna, tells me.

I'm losing it! I reply. Help me! But I know she can't. For us to heal, we'd have to surround ourselves in fire, and that might light the entire forest and bring us unwanted attention.

"Terraemotus!" I order.

Jupiter glances back at me, bobbing his head. He lowers to the forest floor and the ground shakes, threatening to open up. I hear him growl and the powerful earthquake rattles the ground.

I scream as I feel myself roll down a hill I didn't see before. And then it becomes steeper, and steeper, until it's nearly a cliff. "Jupiter!" I call as I fall down. "Stop messing with the terrain!"

The ground stops shaking and then I'm hitting it. Hard. A sharp crack echoes off the trees and everything goes dark.

Chapter Two

"Here, take Jupiter — I'll find another way out." My sister tells me, passing me my baby brother. I situate him on my hip, careful not to burn him with the flame in my hand.

"But what if—" I try to protest. She shakes her head at me, blue curls bouncing.

"Run, and don't stop. When you reach the surface, head to the woods, out of the mountains. But stay away from Wolves"

The walls shake and we duck away from falling loose stones. My eyes well up and I throw my arms around her. "What if you don't make it out?"

She hugs me back tightly. "I promise I'll try, okay?" I nod against Aislee's chest and we both jump as another hit comes. "Take care of Jupiter if I don't make it." I nod again and pull away. "Te amo." She tell me, sadness dripping into her voice.

"Te quoque amo." I give her a long, sad look before turning and crawling through the tiny tunnel. I know there's a high chance I'll never see her again.

I hold onto my one-year-old brother tightly, crawling through the blockade on my knees. I ignore the pain as tiny pebbles penetrate my skin.

When I make it out on the other side, I yell back through the tunnel, in case Aislee's still there. "I made it!"

I take off running then, following her directions. But I'm confused. Mama said avoid the woods, Aislee said run to them.

I shake off the doubt and navigate down the corridor, keeping the balled up fabric in my palm lit with fire.

When I reach the surface, I extinguish it and throw the scrap to the dirt. Peering around, I widen my eyes.

Across the rocky terrain, near the main entrance to the Caves, a warrior line of dragons fights an army. I can make out Wolves and humans, the humans armed and firing at the mountain. The dragons do their best to defend our home.

Baby Jupiter begins to cry, so I take off, wanting to avoid detection. I attempt to run as fast as I can, having trouble as I'm only eleven and carrying a one-year-old baby.

I reach the other secret entrance, knowing this would be where Aislee would come out. The ground rumbles and I nearly drop the baby.

Rocks tumble a few feet deep into the tunnel, blocking it off completely.

"Nullum!" I shriek, and tears flow down my face. I know now for sure that I'll never see Aislee again. Whether she was trapped or dead, my sister was gone, I was running out of time, and I needed to leave her behind.

I wake with a gasp, my eyes wide as I bring myself back from the depths of my memory. I sit up, yelping a little from the graze on my arm. I glance around before my eyes land on Jupiter. His teary blue eyes brighten.

"You're awake!" He exclaims.

"What happened?" I ask groggily. But the second the words leave my mouth, everything rushes back. I wheeze as I realize my baby brother saved my life. He's only five.

"You've been asleep for more than a day." His words choke in his throat; he's trying not to cry. "You aren't healing. I'm scared." A tear trailed down his pale cheek.

I open my arms, wincing from the slight sting. He falls into them, hugging me tightly. "I was so scared, Ry! I didn't know if you'd wake up!" He sobs.

"Shhh." I rub his back, letting him cry. He went through a lot today, for a five year old. He's probably exhausted.

He climbs onto my lap and I gasp, not expecting the sudden pain.

"Sorry!" Jupiter squeals. "I forgot. I think your leg is broken."

I gently lift him off my lap and lean forward, examining the leg. I can't move it; if I try, excruciating pain shoots up to my hips. I lift my tunic up to my mid-thigh and sigh, leaning against a tree.

Dried, sticky blood covers the calf — from where the arrow hit me — but on my thigh, just above the knee, a deep bruise has formed. I know that's where the break is.

I need to heal!

Not unless you want the whole forest on fire! Kenna growls.

"Can you heal?" Jupiter whispers.

I shake my head. "I'll have to heal the slow way. Which means we're stuck here. Sorry buddy."

He shrugged. "I'll take care of you, Ry. If the bad men come back, I'll fight again. Just like before!"

I smile at his energy. "Thanks, Buddy. I can't believe your powers are strong enough!"

He grins, "Yeah! Watch!" He lifts his palms and little bolts of lightning shoots out. His eyes flash yellow and the earth lightly grumbles.

"Did you feel that?" An airy voice gasps from through the trees.

I freeze, gripping Jupiter's arm in mine and stopping whatever power he was about to show me. "Shh." I whisper.

"Was that an earthquake?" A different voice asks. This voice was much deeper.

"It felt so much like one!" The first voice sounds in awe. "But that wouldn't make any sense, right?"

The voices' owners come into view and I attempt to scramble up, yelling as pain bolts through my leg. I crumple back down and the couple stop their conversation, staring in bewilderment at us.

I don't hesitate. I know I can't get up, but there's a chance Jupiter will make it. "Curre." I command softly. He shakes his head, blue eyes wide.

"I'll fight." He whispers. "I'll protect you!"

I shake my head, and then still again when Kenna gains my attention. Wolves.

I begin to panic, my breathing becoming labored as I try to figure out what to do. I study the wolves, getting a sense of how dangerous they are.

There is only two of of them, that I know of. One is a woman, and the other is a man. Both look to be about twenty. I'm sure they're older than that, but werewolf aging confuses me.

Both have dark hair and light eyes; if they were dragons, they'd be Earth. The woman puts her hands out, obviously recognizing my panic.

"Relax." She tells me. "It's okay, we won't hurt you."

I keep unblinking eyes on her, and I feel Jupiter grip my shoulder.

"You're hurt," she states the obvious. "We can help you."

"The wolf is the enemy, they can't be trusted." My mother's words echo in my mind. And then Aislee's: "Stay away from wolves."

I scoot backwards, but only a few inches; a tree blocks my escape route.

"Curre." I tell Jupiter.

"Nullum." He replies.

The couple look confused, unsure of what to do. "Please let us help you! We can take you to a doctor, that leg doesn't look good."

I shake my head. I can heal myself. I think. Stupid trees would burn though!

The woman looks at the man. "I don't want to freak her out anymore." She whispers, "But she's only a child, and the boy with her looks like he hasn't eaten in weeks."

The man nods and they step closer carefully. I yelp when I accidentally move my leg. The couple glance at each other, worry flashing in their eyes.

"I know you're scared," the man says. "But we can get you medical help, and food, and a bed to rest in. You don't have to stay long, just enough to get better."

Jupiter nudges me, I know he's hungry and the offer sounds intriguing, but I have to keep him safe. Wolves are not safe.

"Lupi." I warn as he takes a step towards the couple.

He pauses and glanced back at me. "So?"

I sigh. He wouldn't know. He's too young, mom wouldn't have been able to warn him.

"I'm starving." He whispers, and I'm not sure if he's talking to me or to the wolves.

The woman smiles at him. "We can get you food. And clean clothes."

"Clothes?" He asks, glancing at me. I point to my tunic and he lights up, nodding at the woman. She reaches a hand out and he tentatively takes it. My heart thuds, waiting for them to hurt him, run off with him, anything that tells me everything I've been taught about Wolves is true.

But the woman just picks him up with a gentleness only a mother has. I stare, puzzled. What do I do? I ask Kenna. I get no answer. Maybe she's as startled as I am.

I try to move closer to them, but I'm crippled, unable to get up or even scoot.

"My sister needs help." Jupiter tells the woman. "She can't walk; her leg is broken."

The man nods and walks over to me. I watch him carefully, unsure what he's going to do.

"May I pick you up?" He asks. "We'll take care of you, I promise."

When I don't answer, he glances over to his mate and my brother. "Can she understand English?"

Jupiter nods, his eyes getting heavy. I was right before, he's utterly exhausted.

The man asks me again, and this time I give a timid nod. He smiles warmly and crouches down and snakes an arm behind my back. He's gentle and slow, but it hurts so bad I want to scream. When he gets his other arm beneath my legs and lifts, the pain is so harrowing, I pass out almost instantly, giving myself up to the darkness.

Chapter Three

When I come around, I can't open my eyes, but I can feel and hear everything around me.

I'm lying on some sort of bed. A cot maybe, but it feels softer than that. A blanket is over top of me, covering me from my neck to my knees. My injured leg seems to be up in the air.

The pain is gone, and for that I am grateful. I don't think I'd be able to take much more at this point.

The room I am in is quiet, but bright. Artificial light from above me beams on the other side of my eyelids. I wish I could open my eyes to understand what it was. It definitely isn't the sun, and it's not hot or flickering like fire.

I hear the tapping of shoes on the floor and snap my ears' attention to them.

"Why is she still asleep?" I hear Jupiter squeak. I want to sit up and give him a hug. I try to move, but only a finger is able to even twitch.

"I don't know, honey." I recognize the voice of the woman from the woods. "It's been days, she should be up soon."

Days? I've been asleep for days? This couldn't be happening. I don't even know where I am! I feel my heart begin to race and a beeping from the right speeds up.

"She's awake." A new voice says from the left. I hear the person stand up. "She's panicking."

"I can help her!" Jupiter exclaims, and then I hear little footsteps run towards me.

"Wait!" The woman calls. "She just needs to rest. She'll calm down after a second."

"Nullum." He tells her sharply, although I'm not sure she understands him.

A little hand is placed in mine and instantly I grab onto it. "Soror." He whispers. "Can you hear me?" I squeeze his hand. "I'll let you open your eyes."

I brace myself. The last time he gave me energy, he didn't know how to fully control his power, and I ended up flying three meters.

I'm surprised when it doesn't come as a blast, but more like a gentle wave. I breathe in deeply, sucking in the energy. I feel it travel through my arm to my chest, circulating down to my feet and back up to my other arm. And then finally to my head. The only place it doesn't touch is my raised leg. My eyes flutter open and he stops.

"Gratias tibi." I tell him. He smiles and gives me a hug.

"Te gratissimum." He answers. "I got scared. Non sciunt quid faciunt!"

A tear leaked from my eye. "Et bene." I tried to reassure him. "Nunc huc me." He nods and squeezes me harder.

"They're speaking Latin!" An astonished voice said from next to me. It was the same voice that announced I was panicking before. I turn my head to see a middle aged man in blue clothes and a long white coat. His hair is slightly greying, and his green eyes are kind.

I take a moment to scan the rest of my environment. I am in fact, lying on a cot-like bed, and the blanket that covers me is a deep purple. Odd machines are on both sides of me, a few cords trail from them, attaching to my arm and chest. The floor is white and the walls are a light blue. I can't look at the ceiling, the strange lights are too bright; they hurt my eyes.

My eyes finally land on the woman from the woods. She is sitting in a chair against the wall, watching me with wide eyes. She glances back and forth between my brother and me.

"H-how. . . What just. . ." She clears her throat. "How did he do that?"

Jupiter opens his mouth but I shook him a stern look. "Nullum."

"I'm not allowed to tell you." He says to the woman. She looks at the older man, but he just shrugs.

"Can you at least tell us your names?"

Jupiter glances at me and I give him a surprised look. "I was waiting for you to wake up. In case you didn't want me to tell them." He answers my unspoken question. I smile and give him a nod. He beams and looks back at the woman.

"My name is Jupiter! Like the Roman God of lightning!" My brother announces proudly.

The woman smiles at him and then turns to me. "And your sister?"

"Azari." I tell her; it's the first thing I've said to her.

Her entire face lights up. "That's such a pretty name!"

"Thank you." I whisper.

She stands up and walks over to me, motioning to the man in the blue and white "Azari, this is Doctor Green." The man gives me a smile and a wave. "I'm Jasmin, and the man who carried you here is Cole. He's my ma–husband."

I give her a small smile, but I don't miss her mistake. She was going to say Mate. Which means she thinks we're humans. Good.

Jasmin looks at Doctor Green. "Now that she's awake, can I bring her home?"

The man nods, handing her a piece of paper. "Sign here, and call me if there's any complications. You might also want to let the Addams know you're taking care of them. We don't want to raise unnecessary alerts."

She takes a pen and gracefully drags it across the bottom of the paper. "I will. Thank you so much!"

He nods, "Of course." He stands up and leaves the room, taking the paper with him.

Jasmin gently grabs my hand and I flinch, not expecting that. "Sorry!" She squeaks, retracting her hand. "Because you were out so long, I think it's better we use a wheelchair rather than crutches."

I don't know what either of those words mean. In the Caves, when some-one got hurt, all they had to do was go outside and surround themselves in their element and they were healed. I wish there was a place to do that here. I don't like the hard white substance that is encased around my entire leg. I know they're trying to help, but this really sucks.

"Cole's at home with our son," Jasmin says to me as she helps me sit up. I think she's just trying to awkwardly fill the silence. "Your brother insisted on seeing you." Jupiter grins and she turns to him. "Jupiter, honey, will you get the wheelchair?" He looks confused, so she adds, "the black chair thing with wheels." He scampers over to it and pushes it to the bed.

"Tell me if this hurts you, okay?" I nod, bracing myself, and Jasmin lifts me from the bed, placing me in the weird chair thing. Surprisingly, it didn't hurt. I have a feeling it has something to do with the tube to my arm.

"Whoops," Jasmin chuckles, following my line of sight. "He forgot the IV."

She walks to the other side of me and pulls out the tube and needle. She places a small bandage over the spot and smiles at me. "Better?" I nod, and she goes behind me and pushes the chair. It rolls towards the doorway and Jupiter walks next to me, holding my hand.

"Ready to go home?" Jasmin asks enthusiastically.

Jupiter jumps in the air. "Yes!" But all I can do is stare straight ahead of me. What am I getting myself into?

Chapter Four

The sun is bright, but familiar, as Jasmin pushes me onto the sidewalk. Apparently they walked here, so now we're walking to her house.

The building we came out of is big, and simple. It's built of brick and has windows along the front and sides of it. The roof is flat on top. I think I heard Jasmin call it a Doctor's Office. But if she's a Werewolf, wouldn't we go to the Pack Doctor?

She pushes me down the sidewalk in silence, occasionally saying something to Jupiter. I take this time to observe where we are.

Next to the flat-roofed building is another big structure, but this one has a pointed roof and isn't as big. A wide, roofed patio with picnic tables circles it. I want to keep my speaking to a minimal, but my curiosity overcomes me.

"What is that?" I point to the building I've been studying.

Jasmin stops the wheelchair so we can look at the structure some more. "That is the Lodge. We eat group meals there sometimes and that's where meetings are held." I nod and she continues walking. What she meant is Pack meetings and dinners are held there.

I look to the left, across the street, where a row of modest-size houses sit. Except for one; the one closest to the Doctor's Office.

This one is different. It's slightly bigger and has two people standing outside the door. The people are rigid, unmoving. Like soldiers.

Jasmin must see me staring, because then she says: "That's our group leaders' house." The Alpha's. That would explain the guards.

The curtains on the second level swish and I swear I see dark hair flash behind the window. I blink and it's gone.

I return to observing my surroundings. Every house looks similar, but with their own styles and gardens put in. Peering between houses, I notice more rows. It seems as though the houses circle around the Alpha's house, the Doctor's, and the Lodge. The format kind of looks like a target, I guess.

We turn down a few different nameless streets and I start picturing it in my head. The target format of houses. It's like some kind of neighborhood and kind of reminds me how the Caves worked. But the Caves were under a mountain. This is a neighborhood. A Wolf Pack neighborhood.

"Here we are!" Jasmin says suddenly, pushing me up a concrete path much wider than the normal sidewalk. The house we're going towards is two stories high and painted pale blue. The shutters and trim are white, along with the front door. I smile a little; it's cute.

Jasmin stops at the top of the wide sidewalk. We've come to a white wall that's different than the house siding. I'm not entirely sure why it's different. Until she punches in a code and the wall moves. I jump, not expecting that.

The white wall makes a rickety noise as it climbs towards the roof, disappearing into wall above. I stare, completely fascinated.

Jasmin giggles at my expression, "Have you ever seen a garage door before?"

I don't answer, I just watch until it comes to a stop. Jasmin pushes me inside and I find out the wall didn't disappear, it just folded backwards and was just sitting against the ceiling. I don't know what to make of that.

Jasmin stops at steps leading to a white door. She opens it and calls inside. "Cole! Will you come help me?"

The man from the woods appears and helps lift me through the doorway. I wish they'd just let me heal the fast way.

Inside, the house is beautiful, decorated carefully and wonderfully. Through an open door next to the garage entrance, I see a small bathroom. On the other side of the short hallway is a closet. It holds coats and shoes. The only thing that bothers me is that the place smells like wolf. I guess I'll have to get used to that.

Wait, what?

I backtrack my thoughts, reminding myself that we're not staying. The first opportunity that arises, we're out of here.

A flash of guilt stabs my heart though. I was starting to enjoy Jasmins company. Not quite to a comfortable level, but still.

"Because of your injured leg, I thought it would be best to have your room be on the main floor, that way you don't have to deal with stairs." She pauses, waiting for my reaction. I nod, and she continues. "I didn't know what you like, so I just did neutral. But we can change anything if you don't like it!" She adds quickly, pushing me down a hallway. "Don't be afraid to tell me if you don't like something. I want you to be comfortable."

She stops in a doorway and I suck in a breath. The room is gorgeous, and not to mention huge. Through a big window on the right, I can see the front yard, and a small child playing in the grass across the street.

A queen bed is on the left, sticking out into the room from a smaller window that views the backyard. The bedspread is white, with little scrunches dotting it to give it fluff and texture. Red and black accent pillows are thrown on top.

The walls are painted a very light grey and the curtains on either side of the front yard window are white, matching the bedspread.

My favorite part, though, is the reading corner. A wide bookshelf runs along the entire far wall, practically filling the entire space. And from the ceiling, an odd, bubble-like chair hangs. It sort of looks like a cocoon. I desperately want to run to it and curl up to read. I'll have to do that sometime later.

"Do you like it?" Jasmin asks. She sounds nervous, as if she's worried I'll hate it.

She shouldn't be worried, though. I freaking loved it! I twisted my head around and beamed at her. "I love it!" I breathed.

She fiddles with her hands, "Are you sure? Because we can change anything you want. The color of the walls, the bedspread, the pillows. . . I picked red because you seem to like red. Your dress thing was dyed red and you have that red bracelet—"

I giggle and touch her hand, making her go still. She blinks down at me. "I don't want to change anything." I whisper.

She smiles, still seeming nervous. I realize she must be new at this. She mentioned having a son, but he must still be young.

"Oh!" She gasps, pushing me further into the room. "Over here, is your bathroom. And here, is your closet." On the same wall as the doorway, two more doors led to dark spaces.

"There's a few outfits in the closet for you. They're old clothes of mine and they probably won't fit you right. But don't worry, I can take you shopping soon for your own stuff." She rambles, "Ooh! And we can get you makeup and shoes and hair things!"

I wince, hopefully unnoticeably. Did she think I was staying here forever? I don't want to make her feel bad — she seemed so excited!

"Well I'll leave you to get settled, holler if you need anything. I'll come get you for dinner, alright?" I give her a nod and she leaves the room.

I sigh, alone at last. I wheel myself over to the front yard window and peer out. My heart skips a beat when I realize my direct line of sight leads to the Alpha's home. It's a few streets away, but I can see a few windows through the spaces between other houses. That's not what made my heart skip, though. It was the emerald green eyes staring right back at me.

Chapter Five

I roll away from the window, my heart pounding. Who was that? Why were they staring at me? For some reason, my heart longed to see who those bright green eyes belonged to.

You're being stupid! I scold myself. I shake my head to clear it and focus my attention to my injured leg. I wish there were another way to heal it that didn't have to do with fire.

I growl in frustration, staring at the cast that is supposed to protect the leg from further damage. Heal! I order it. Kenna chuckles from inside my head and now I'm angry. Shut up, I'm trying everything I can!

I think I'm staring too hard because the next thing I know, the cast is in flames. I curse under my breath and quickly put it out. I slump back in my chair feeling hopeless. I'm about to try again when a knock on the door makes me jump. I don't say anything and eventually the door cracks open. I'm surprised to see a little boy standing there; and it's not my brother.

"Um, Momma said supper is ready." He doesn't look me in the eye, and he sounds incredibly nervous. I give him a small smile and roll to the door. "Follow me." He says.

The little boy leads me down the hallway and turns to the right, where the room opens and a table is being set by Cole. The boy shows me to a seat and I get out of the chair thingy and hop on one leg to it, plopping back down. I'm surprised and slightly concerned how much energy that took. I've become weak.

Jasmin brings over a big pot of something that smells incredible. I think it's soup. "Jupiter!" She calls and I can hear the sound of little feet pounding down the stairs. He slides into a spot across from me. The boy from earlier sits next to me and Jasmin and Cole sit at the table's ends.

"Help yourselves." Jasmin tells us, "It's chicken noodle soup. And this is garlic bread." She points to the pot and then to a pan of bread that I didn't notice before.

I tentative take a piece of bread and place it on my place. "Gracias tibi." I say, and then feel my face go red as I realize I forgot to speak English.

Jasmin smiles, "Does that mean 'thank you'?" I blush harder and nod. "Well, I don't know Latin for 'you're welcome,' but you're very welcome. Would you like some soup?"

I nod again and hand her my bowl. She scoops some of the stuff from the pot into the bowl. She hands it back and I take a deep breath, concentrating with my senses to figure out what's in it.

The broth has a savory, salty tang to it and matches whatever meat is in the soup. I'm not familiar with the meat, but I think she mentioned it was something called chicken. I don't think I've ever had chicken.

Back home at the Caves, we mostly ate fish, occasionally turkey, mountain lion, goat, and stuff we can make with certain grains and milk.

I take a bite and immediately sigh. It was as good as it smelled. Jasmin giggles at my reaction. "You like it?" I nod vigorously before practically inhaling the rest of the bowl. I also haven't eaten in days!

I finish the bread as well and then turn to Jasmin. "Can I go to bed?" I ask softly.

She looks surprised I even talked at all, but then she nods. "Of course, honey. The more you rest, the better that leg will get."

I halfheartedly smile. Or, I think. I could just heal myself the easy way.

I help myself into my wheelchair, after declining Cole's offer to help, and wheel myself back to my room.

My room.

That feels weird. I haven't been able to call a place my own since the Caves. Not going to lie, it felt good. It feels even better to crawl into bed and under the covers.

I'm amazed at how comfortable the bed is, and I don't even bother to change out of my tunic or close the blinds. Instead, I go right to sleep.

Chapter Six

"Rise and shine." A voice stirs me from my dreams. Honestly, I'm thankful; they weren't so much dreams as they were nightmares.

I blink open my eyes and turn my head to the right, where I see Jasmin standing in the doorway. Her eyes look apologetic.

"I'm sorry, normally I'd let you sleep in, especially with that injury, but we have company coming over and thought you might want to be up when they get here."

I push myself into a sitting position and blink at her. Visitors?

"Remember the group leader I mentioned before? He wants to meet you. Mostly for security reasons, but nothing to worry about," she answers my unspoken question. "He has a daughter about your age, maybe you could get to know someone here?"

I shrug; I'm not sure she really knows how old I am. I'm pretty small for my age and breed of dragon. Usually Fire and Earth are the ones with a bigger, stronger build than Water and Wind have. I'm fifteen, but I look eleven or twelve. It's pathetic, really.

"I have a cute sundress you can wear, and then maybe after they leave we can go shopping for clothes that actually fit you." Jasmin smiles and I force one back. I'm not sure exactly what shopping is, but it doesn't sound fun.

"For now," she continues, "you can borrow my things." I think she's forgotten she already told me all of this yesterday. "If you want to shower, soap and shampoo is already in there, and your cast is waterproof, so you should be all set! Let me know if you need anything." She gives me a wide smile and shuts the door, leaving me to get up and ready.

It may be water proof. I think to myself. But is it fire proof?

I swing my legs over the side of the bed and carefully place my feet to the carpet. I find I can put weight on the injured leg, but I can't walk on it yet. It's healing faster on its own than I expected.

I hop on one foot to the bathroom and open the door, flicking on the light switch. My eyes pop out of their sockets.

The bathroom is so breathtaking, it's hard to describe. The tiles are perfectly polished and seem to sparkle back at me. The shower curtain is a faded red color with a flame design embroidered across it.

A flicker of fear shoots through my mind. Does she know? I shake my head. How could she? She thinks I'm human, and I'd like it to stay that way for as long as I can.

The sink counter is a pretty white and grey marble-like stone that matches the tiled floor so well it's satisfying. The cabinets are black, and the walls are a white-grey.

I close the door and hope across the tile to the shower and slide open the curtain. It takes me a couple minutes to figure out how to work the water, but once it's running I hop back and peel my red tunic off over my head. I'm horrified at what I see in the mirror.

I look like I've been abused.

I'm flat as a board and can see my ribs and my hips stretching through my skin. There are several bruises on my waist, back and shoulders; probably from the fall I had after those Hunters attacked. If Jasmin saw this, I think she's have a heart attack. It's not like I'm her daughter or anything, but she seems overly protective and caring for me already. I shouldn't be complaining though, it's kind of nice to have someone looking after me after being on my own so long.

I open the vanity drawers until I find a brush to rip through the bird's nest that's supposed to be my hair. Once it runs through smoothly, I set it down and hop to the shower.

I take the next ten minutes under the water to basically scrub off the last four years of my life. It feels nice to be actually clean again.

I hobble out and wrap a fluffy red towel around me, my legs nearly buckling. I need to build up my strength. It's not good for Kenna if I'm this weak.

I quickly go to the closet to find a single dress hanging from a rod with undergarments underneath it. I drop the towel and throw the outfit on, not supposed to find everything a bit loose. I'm so tiny.

I hope out of the closet and flop down onto the bed. Getting ready wore me out.

"Azari!" I hear Jasmin call from down the hall. "Do you want breakfast?" I don't want to yell back so I heave myself up and over to the wheeled chair thing and push myself out the door towards the kitchen. Jasmin smiles when she sees me.

"You look beautiful! And I can help you with your hair after you eat." I blinked, I'd forgotten about my hair. Whoops.

Suddenly, panic consumes me as I realize I haven't checked on Jupiter. My head snaps back and forth as I scan the main floor and then I visibly relax when I see him in the living room, playing with Jasmin's son, whose name I have yet to learn.

"He's okay," Jasmin whispers. "You can trust us, you know. I get we're still strangers to you, but maybe if you let your walls down a little, this won't all be so frightening?"

I turn my eyes to her and she places a plate of meat strips and something yellow and fluffy in front of me. 'If you let your walls down...' her words ring in my head and I break our eye contact. I'm not sure I want to do that.

She sighs sadly and I glance back up under my eye lashes. "What do you want to know?" I say so quietly I'm almost not sure she hears me.

Her head snaps towards me and her eyes widen in a "I'm surprised but oh-so-happy" kind of way. "Um," she says as she pulls out the chair across from me. "We can start as small as possible, I guess." I give her a close-lipped smile, unsure of what's coming. "Lets start with 'what's your favorite color?'"

I almost laugh, maybe letting my walls down won't be so bad.

Chapter Seven

"Red." I answer, even though I'm pretty sure she already could guess that. "Rubrum."

She smiles so wide I could count her teeth. "Is that Latin for red?" I nod. "Oh, it's such a pretty word!"

I giggle slightly at her enthusiasm. "I guess. What about you?"

"My favorite color?" She looks startled I asked. "Mine is indigo. Like the night sky."

"Pretty." I whisper.

"How long were you in the woods?"

I freeze, not expecting the topic jump.

"Sorry! That one isn't necessarily on the easy, gentle side, is it? You don't have to answer. Here: what's your favorite animal?"

I open my mouth three of four times before I close my eyes and decide what to say. I have to blurt it before I change my mind.

"Four years."

She blinks until understanding lights up her face. And then sympathy overtakes it. "You were on your own for four years?" I nod in confirmation. She lowers her voice to a whisper, "What happened? Never mind, you don't have to answer that. You've already taken a big step."

"I—" I start when a jarring knock on the front door cuts me off and makes me jump.

"Oh! The Addams are here! Mason, will you get that?" She hops up and then glances at my plate of untouched food with concern. "Are you not hungry?"

I shrug. "What is it?"

She smiles and points to the meat strips first and then the yellow fluff. "That's bacon. It comes from pigs and is fatty and delicious. And those are scrambled eggs. They come from chicken."

Chickens lay eggs. Good to know.

I take a bite of both, deciding I like the eggs better than the meat. I think I just miss the meat from home.

"Hello, Mason." A deep voice makes my head snap to the front door.

I see Jasmin's son dip his head in a slight bow. "Alpha." He runs back over to Jupiter, sitting down beside him.

"Hello!" Jasmin says cheerily as she reaches the front door where four people have come into view.

There are two girls and two boys. It's obvious that two are the parents and two are their children. This must be the Alpha Family. I make no move to push myself over there. I just observe from my spot at the table.

Jasmin leads them to the living room and they take a seat on the couches. She offers them drinks, and they all ask for waters.

The family looks strikingly similar to each other, each kid taking after one parent. They all have silky, raven black hair and fairly pale skin. However, while the parents have deep, dark eyes, their children have neither. The girl has pretty ice blue eyes, but I can't get a good look at the boy's.

The boy is taller than his parents, and very well built. The girl is taller than I would be standing up, and she's got muscle, but she's still on the petite side.

The girl smiles at my brother, showing pearly white teeth. She tries to talk to him but he keeps his mouth tightly shut and his eyes neutral. I hold in a chuckle.

Jasmin returns to the living room with the waters and sits in a chair across from them. No one seems to acknowledge me yet.

"I'm glad you brought your children! I think Kiara might be around Azari's age. It'll be good for her to meet people outside of the doctor's and this house."

The girl — who I'm assuming is Kiara — looks around the room, her eyes landing on me. She smiles and gets up, ignoring her father's command to sit still. I focus on her and I don't get to hear the rest of what Jasmin is saying.

The girl pulls out the chair next to me and sits down. Her eyes are bright and excited as she extends a hand to me.

"Hi! I'm Kiara. You must be Azari."

I tentatively take her hand and give it a small shake. I'm not sure what to say. She seems super perky. Like another level of Jasmin. I settle on "Hi."

"I don't know if anyone's told you this before, but gosh, you are just gorgeous!"

I touch the ends of my fire-red hair, suddenly self-conscious as I remember Jasmin never did it. "Thanks." I whisper.

She tilts her head, her eyes sparkling a little. "You don't talk much, do you? Well that's okay, I guess. People tell me all the time that I talk too much, so I might just do enough talking for the both of us!" She laughs and I give her a small smile.

"Kiara!" Her father barks from the couch. "What are you doing?"

Kiara stands up. "Making a friend." She replies in a "duh!" tone. I notice her mother gives her a stern look.

"Kiara, we don't know her yet. She could be dangerous. That's why we're here."

Kiara rolls her eyes at me and I bite back a giggle. "She seems pretty okay to me!" She leans down to whisper, "Can I push you to the living room?" I nod and she pulls me away from the table and over to the living room.

I catch Kiara's brother's eye and hold back a gasp. Those were the same vibrant green eyes that I'd seen through the window the first day.

I realize the world has stopped around me, and I can't hear Kiara arguing with her parents anymore. All I can see is him and for some reason, my eyes won't tear themselves away. I notice we both stopped breathing for a minute.

Finally, I'm able to blink and whatever just happened breaks. No one seems to catch it, but every time I glance to him, his eyes are still glued to me.

"Azari, is it?" Kiara's father asks loudly, making me jump and break eye contact with his son. After a second, I nod. "Jasmin tells me she found you and your brother all alone. Why is that?" I suck in a breath, not wanting to speak to the stranger.

Jasmin jumps in. "I don't think interrogating her is the best—"

The Alpha holds up his hand, cutting her off. "I'm just getting a feel for who she is." He turns back to me and repeats his question, and even though Jasmin was trying to save me from answering, I can see she's genuinely curious as well.

"I- we-" I stutter before stopping and letting out a sigh. "We had to run."

The Alpha's eyebrows shoot up. "Run?" I give him a nod. "Run from where? Or should I say who?"

I look at my lap, where I'm fiddling with my fingers. "My home was being attacked. We had to escape. I don't wanna talk about it."

He nods in understanding, but his eyes tell me he wants more. I'm not going to give him more.

The Alpha suddenly lightly slaps his leg and stands up, making both Jupiter and me jump. "Well, I think it's safe for you to take care of them, but just know I'll like to stop by often and hopefully learn a little bit more about each, if that's alright." Jasmin nods. As if she'd ever say no to her Alpha. "Kiara, Bryce, let's go."

He and his wife begin walking to the door, but Kiara and the boy I now know as Bryce stay behind a minute. Jasmin jumps up and grins at Kiara as if she just got the most brilliant idea.

"Kiara! Would you mind taking Azari shopping today? She needs clothes of her own and I don't want to have to drag the boys there too."

I don't think I've ever heard someone squeal as loud as Kiara just did. I cringe and Bryce lightly slaps his sister's shoulder.

"I would love to! Oh My Gosh, it'll be so much fun! I know ALL the best stores!" She chuckles sheepishly, "If you can't tell, I love shopping." She glances at her brother. "Ooh, and Bryce could come with us and be our bag carrier!" Bryce groans and I widen my eyes. "Mom, Dad, is that okay?"

The Alpha Female shrugs. "I don't see why not. But take a couple guards with you."

Kiara groans, but nods her head. "Fine. It'll still be fun." She leans close to me so her parents can't hear, "We'll just ditch 'em!"

I smile half-heartedly, not completely sure what I'm getting myself into.

"So, are you ready?"

I give a timid nod, although I think I'm trying to convince myself more than Kiara.

Chapter Eight

Kiara leads me outside — Bryce helps with pushing my chair — to what I think will be our transportation. It's a long, sleek black thing with windows and doors. It sits on wheels and is growling like an oversized dog.

Suddenly, a man pops out of nowhere and opens one of the back doors. He helps me out of the chair and Bryce gently lifts me into the machine. My face heats up like a ball of fire and my stomach does backflips.

Kiara climbs in after us and sits down in a plush seat across from me. I blush even harder as I realize Bryce had chosen to stay immediately to my left. I try not to dwell on that fact and instead look around at the contraption we're in.

There's a row of seats on each side, and I estimate they can fit about three people. Darkened windows line the wall above. That's where we're sitting; Bryce and me on one side, and Kiara across the tiny aisle.

On the far ends of the narrow room are two more seats. Neither have windows above them, but on the left side of me, the seats back up against a half-wall and I can see the man who opened the door now sitting on the other side, facing the front.

Kiara giggles and I snap my attention to her. "Have you never been in a car before?" I shake my head. I didn't even know that's what it was called! "Well, this is a Limo, it's bigger and nicer than most cars. We prefer to travel this way; it's more comfortable." I nod, not sure what to say.

Kiara slides down her bench of seats, reaching for the wall at the end. She flips a tiny switch and colored lights dance across the ceiling. My mouth forms an O shape and my eyes brighten. Kiara giggles again.

And then we move. I gasp, not expecting that. It's not a jerking motion, however. Instead, it's a nice smooth transition. I glance to the front and realize the man from before is controlling the car. That would make him the Driver.

I lean back in my seat and stare at the lights above me. A sudden question pops into my mind, but I don't want to ask it. They'll think I'm incredibly stupid. Which I guess I am in a sense. I know next to nothing about the world I've been tossed into.

An elbow nudge from my left makes me blink up at Bryce.

"What's on your mind?" He asks softly. "Don't be afraid to speak your thoughts. We're here to help in any way we can."

I glance at Kiara and she gives me a smile and a nod. I sigh as I hesitate. "What's. . . Shopping?"

Kiara gasps dramatically and her brother widens his forest-green eyes. I blush furiously and duck my head, hiding behind a fiery curtain of hair.

"Sorry," Kiara says, getting me to glance up at her. "It's just, you don't know what shopping is?"

I shrug, and my face probably matches my hair at this point. "I've never done it."

Kiara grasps my hands in hers, balancing on the edge of her seat. "Well, it's only like, one of the best things in the world!" I smile at her enthusiasm, even if it's kind of scaring me a little. "It's like where you can go to get whatever you need, for money of course, but that's not an issue in our Pack. I like going for clothes the most, but you can get accessories, clothes, makeup, and even food."

I almost miss the last sentence. She blatantly said they're in a Pack. Does she know I'm not supposed to know?

"Anyway, Jasmin said you needed things of your own, so clothes will be our main priority today. We can always come back just for fun some other time, though!"

"But let us know if you get hungry, there'll always be time to pause and get something to eat." Bryce added. Kiara rolled her eyes at him, but said to me: "Right, of course."

She pauses for a second before randomly blurting out, "Where did your mom come up with your name? It's so unique!"

"Kiara!" Bryce warns, but she ignores him.

An image of when I last saw my mother forms in my head and I have to blink back tears before I can answer. "I'm not sure. But everyone in the Caves have names that wouldn't be so common to you guys."

"The Caves?" Kiara asks and I stretch my eyes wide, running over the sentence in my head.

I'd mentioned the Caves. I realize. I didn't mean to, it just slipped out. It took me a second to recognize why I'd said it so blatantly.

Trust. I trust them. Wolves! I can't believe I'm trusting wolves. Especially ones I met just today. But the strange thing is, I don't regret it. Not one bit.

I like these two. I probably shouldn't yet, but I do. And surprisingly, I'm not afraid of that.

This probably isn't the smartest idea, but this step might as well become a leap.

"That's what we called our home." I barely pause before saying, "Hey, this is going to sound strange, but is there somewhere open we could stop before. . . Shopping? I'd rather not get pushed around in a wheel chair."

Kiara and Bryce stare at me. I don't think they were expecting that many words to come out of my mouth. Kiara gets over it first and gives her head a tiny shake.

"Uh, yeah I think so. Why does it have to be open?"

I decide to be vague now. "It's better if you see for yourself." I really don't want to show them this part of me yet, but I need to heal myself. I don't know how much longer I can handle the wheel chair and cast thing. "Oh, and no trees or anything too flammable."

Kiara blinks at me. "Okay. . ." She leans over to the half wall and says something to the driver. He nods.

Bryce continues to stare at me with mixed emotions. With barely a glance, I can see wonder, astonishment, and confusion written all over his face.

A few moments later, the vehicle we're in slows down to a stop. I look outside the window to see wide area of nothing but dirt, grass, and rock. The road we are on seems pretty vacant of other cars. "Perfectus."

Kiara suddenly looks nervous as the driver opens the door. "You aren't planning on like, killing us or anything, right?"

I blink at her. "No! I'm going to heal."

"Heal?" Bryce asks, coming to his senses and helping me out of the car.

I nod, hobbling on one foot a few feet away. I turn to look back at them. "Please don't hate me after this, I'd never intentionally hurt you after all the hospitality you guys have shown." They give me confused looks. "And if you figure things out, please don't lock me up right away. . . I'll explain everything if you want me to." I cringe at my own promise. Aislee would be disappointed in me.

"Azari, what are you talking about?" Kiara whispers, and I almost don't catch it over the wind.

"Please. I can't be broken anymore."

They both give me a timid nod. And I take a deep breath, hopping farther away. I don't want to risk burning them alive.

Kenna! I call into the depths of my mind. We can heal. I hear her gasp excitedly as she pushes her way to the surface. I know my eyes must be glowing now, so I continue facing away from my new friends. I inhale sharply, and then I erupt into flames.

Chapter Nine

I leap back in horror as flames surround my little mate. She doesn't scream, she doesn't call for help. Nothing.

The ball of fire widens slowly and I grip my sister's arm, unsure what's happening. "Azari!" I scream, but my words are lost to the wind.

"Shh!" Kiara snaps, "She said she's healing. And if this is the way, let it happen."

I give her an appalled look. "Let it happen? My mate is surrounded by fire!"

Kiara doesn't answer me, and turns back to the scene. I can feel the heat from here; no wonder she told us to stay back.

So I watch, fighting every instinct that's telling me to save Azari. The fire grows with every second, getting taller and wider. For a split second, I swear I see a dark shadow of something that's definitely not human. And then it's gone. As soon as the fire started, it's put out by an unknown force. Lying still in the aftermath of dust, is the crumpled form of my mate.

"Azari!" Kiara screams and makes a mad dash across the rocky terrain. I make no hesitation to follow her.

She still hasn't moved by the time we reach her, only to find why. She's completely unconscious.

I drop to my knees beside her and grip her hand in mine. It's warm, feverish even. I look up to my sister. "Go tell the driver we need to turn back. I'll carry her to the car." Kiara nods and takes off again.

I gently get my left arm under her shoulders and my right behind her knees. I lift her up, to find she's insanely light. I mean, when she stood up, she was smaller than I expected, but this makes me think she might've been malnourished before meeting Jasmin.

I rush my mate back to the limo, where the driver is waiting with the vehicle still on. Kiara climbs in after me, shutting the door. The second we sit, we're moving.

I hold Azari tight to me and look at my sister. "What. Just. Happened."

Her eyes are as wide as I know mine are. She reaches a hand out and touches my mate's hand. She flinches back, "She's hot still. Did she create the fire?"

I look down at Azari's still form, trying to wrap my head around what she did. "What is she?"

Kiara goes still at my question. "Not a wolf. Not a human."

A word flashes across my brain but I shove it out immediately. No. Not my mate.

I sigh, "I have a theory about the whole situation, though."

Kiara perks up. "What do you mean?"

I move my attention to the world wizzing by out the window. "I don't think she ever planned on going shopping. I think this was her way out, away from house so she could. . . heal."

My sister tilts her head. "You mean, she knew she would go unconscious afterwards? She never intended on making it all the way to the mall?"

I nod. "I think she didn't really want us to see what she could do. But her mind knew it was the only time she could get to an open enough area." I chuckle, "I'm glad she didn't just do that at home. She would've burned the whole pack down!"

Kiara doesn't answer, only gives me a slight nod. And soon enough, we're pulling back up into Jasmin's driveway. I'm glad my parents are gone, we don't need an interrogation.

The driver hurriedly hops out and bolts around the side to open the door for us. I climb out first, keeping Azari close to my chest. Kiara follows closely as we rush up the front steps and the door is opened.

Jasmin's pale as a ghost.

"Oh my goodness! What happened? Here, bring her to the couch."

I hear a wail and see Kiara scooping up a young boy. He fights her, reaching out for Azari. "Ry! Ry! What did you do to her?"

I gently lay my mate on the couch and step back, letting Jasmin take a look.

I hear a thud and turn to see the boy clumsily escape Kiara's hold. He barrels towards me, intent on getting to Azari. I catch him with one arm, lifting him up and holding him still so he can see my face.

"Hey! Hey, it's okay! Azari is just sleeping for a little bit okay?"

He stops fighting me, but fat tears continue rolling down his cheeks. After a few moments, his blurry eyes find mine. "She looks dead! I can't have both sisters die!"

I share a glance with Kiara, who covers her mouth and looks like she's about to cry herself.

I sit down and settle the child on my lap. I get him to look at me again, "Hey, don't worry about that, okay? Azari won't die. I promise. She just needs to rest for a second."

He nods and wipes his tears with his hands. He takes shaky breaths and then looks back into my eyes. "Why is my sissy sleeping? Did she fall?"

I shake my head, about to say something that would calm him down more, but then an idea hit me. I bet he knows. "Buddy, what's your name?"

"Jupiter."

I nod, "Jupiter, your sister burst into flames and now she's sleeping. Do you know anything about this?"

Jupiter widens his eyes, his face draining any color. "I-I'm not supposed to-to tell you."

I look over at Kiara and she walks over, squatting down next to us. Without looking, I know Jasmin is listening as well.

"Has she done this before?" Kiara asks the kid.

He nods. "When she's hurt, and sometimes when she's shifting." He slaps his hands over his mouth. "Whoops." He mumbles.

He scrabbles off my lap and scurries away towards the stairs. I hear his footsteps racing as he climbs and then it goes silent. No one goes after him.

"She's a wolf."

I snap my head to Jasmin, who looks even more pale. I notice her hands are shaking.

"She's a wolf. And she knows this is a pack of them. And she didn't say anything."

I stand up, getting her attention. "She's not a wolf."

"What?"

"She can't be a wolf. I mean, can wolves summon fire like that? Only royals have powers and if she was a Royal, we would've smelled it."

Jasmin nods as she thinks this over. "But then, what is she? We know she's a shifter, thanks to her brother. But what kind?"

A raspy voice snaps my focus to the couch. "Don't."

Chapter Ten

I rapidly blink my eyes as they try to adjust to the harsh light above me. Oh no. I think. Am I back at the Doctor's? I hope not.

When my eyes stop burning and I can see, my other senses flood back as well. I'm under a blanket, but I'm not on a bed. I slightly turn my head and suddenly everything I was just thinking goes out the window.

To the side, in the living room — that means I'm at Jasmin's — stands three figures. Kiara, Jasmin, and Bryce. I zone in and catch the last of Jasmin's sentence.

"-a wolf. She's a wolf and she knows this is a pack of them and she didn't say anything."

I widen my eyes. I think they're talking about me. I think they're trying to figure out what I am.

I know I told Bryce I'd explain everything before I healed myself. But now I regret saying that. I do not want to share my deepest secret to these people. Even if I feel like I have a super strong connection to a certain someone.

"She's not a wolf." I flick my eyes to the said certain someone.

"What?" Jasmin says.

"She can't be a wolf. I mean, can wolves summon fire like that? Only royals have powers and if she was a Royal, we would've smelled it." I flinch at his words. They're figuring it out too fast.

Jasmin nods as she thinks this over. "But then, what is she? We know she's a shifter, thanks to her brother. But what kind?" What? Did Jupiter tell them something?

"Don't." I blurt, coughing as my throat feels like it's coated in gravel.

All heads whip around in shock.

"Azari!" Bryce exclaims, running over to me and gently grabbing my hand. "Are you okay?"

I nod, and I don't pull away from his oddly comforting touch.

Kiara walks over as well while Jasmin dashes to the kitchen. I hear her pour some water into a glass.

Kiara crouches down and I'm forced to look her in the eye. "Don't what, Azari?"

I shake my head slightly. I can't tell them what I am. I may be loosening up and letting down some of my walls, but that's going to far. At least for now. "Don't guess. I won't tell you. I can't."

Kiara sighs in understanding, but I can see it in her eyes that she's dying to know. Bryce keeps quiet, but he squeezes my hand. Sparks shoot up my arm and I widen my eyes at our entwined hands, not expecting that.

I flick my eyes up at Bryce, who is also looking at our hands. "There they are." He whispers.

My mouth drops open; I'm so confused. "There what are?"

Bryce just smiles at me and then a glass of water is placed in front of me. "Thank you," I tell Jasmin and Bryce helps me sit up so I can take a sip. The liquid washes down the gravel feeling and I sigh in content.

Jasmin pulls two chairs over, sitting in one and offering the other to Kiara. When I glance over at her, her face has gone serious.

"Azari, I know it's not natural for you to instantly trust us, and I know you don't want to share what you are, but could you give us something? Anything? We want to get to know you; we want to help."

My eyes flick down to my lap. I don't want to, but I know I need to. I won't share too many details, in case I'll ever get the chance to go home, but I guess I could give them a little something.

"How about your home?" Kiara offers. "In the car you mentioned a place called The Caves. What is that?"

I peek up at her, keeping my voice soft. "My home. The place I was born, where I grew up, where I learned to fight, shift, survive." I pause, thinking about what exactly I should tell them.

"It's like a serious of underground tunnels. Each family has their own quarters. I shared a room with my sister, while Jupiter still slept in my parent's room. Each one of us has special roles, it's a system for the whole community. My father happened to be a leader. My mother was his. . . helper, I guess."

Bryce tilts his head. "You say that in past tense. Is it just because you're not with them anymore?"

I duck my head. Do not get emotional. "I'm pretty sure they're gone."

Kiara covers her mouth, and I know she feels bad for me. I try not to pay attention to her pity.

"Gone? As in. . ."

I nod. "Gone."

Kiara leans over and wraps her arms around me in a tight embrace. A hug I didn't know I needed until she gave it to me. "I'm so sorry! Are you sure that's what happened?"

I nod. "I mean, if they were still here wouldn't they have come looking for us? Wouldn't they have at least tried to find me?"

Bryce squeezes my hand again, and this time I welcome the electricity that circles our fingers.

"And you had to run, because you were being attacked. Right?" Jasmin pipes up.

I nod solemnly, not looking any of them in the eye. "It was wolves." I whisper.

Bryce growls and Jasmin gasps. Kiara looks like she has no idea what to say for once.

"You know, don't you? That's why you told Jupiter to be cautious of us the first day. You're afraid to get close to wolves, and you have a terribly sad, but good reason." She tentatively reaches out and squeezes my arm.

Using the hand that isn't holding mine, Bryce gently grabs my chin and forces me to look him in the eye. "It wasn't us, okay? This pack doesn't attack without an excellent reason. Do you know which pack did that to your. . . Community?" I shake my head and he sighs, letting go of me. "It's probably those mutts from the Altay Peaks Pack."

I shrug, I don't know wolf pack names! I just know we called ourselves the Altai Dragons.

C'mon! Kenna pops up out of nowhere. Just tell them!

No.

Whyyyy? She whines. You know you trust them. And I think you have an idea why, you're just afraid to act on it.

I don't know what you're talking about. I argue.

But you do! She sings back, and I roll my eyes at her.

Kenna!

Look, you know he'll still love you after you reveal your big secret, so might as well just get it over with, yeah?

I sigh at her argument. And then I freeze. Wait, what?!

Chapter Eleven

It's been several weeks since I've healed myself, and I've basically reverted back to my original, guarded self.

Once Kenna made me realize the connection I have with Bryce was more than I thought it was, I've been scared. I still have the dream to one day go home, but if I get close to him, it might not be so easy.

At the moment, I'm lying in my bed, staring at the ceiling, and thinking about Bryce.

Ugh! Stop it! I tell myself.

Admit it! Kenna growls at me. You like him!

No! I snap. I can't like him! It'll change everything!

Change can be good. My dragon argues.

What if I get to go home? That shuts her up. As much as she likes Bryce, she wants to go home even more.

There's been a few times I've had the opportunity to grab Jupiter and run, but Kenna always flashes a picture through my mind of one of these wolves I've grown quite fond of: Jasmin, Kiara, Bryce, and even little Mason.

Ugh, what is happening to me? Why can't my life go back to normal? Well the normal I'd gotten used to for the last four years.

After a few more minutes, I pull back my covers and roll out of bed. I run my fingers through my tangly hair and — using a hair tie from my wrist — I sweep the red strands into a messy bun.

I open my bedroom door and lightly walk to the dining room. An incredible smell I've come to recognize as these flat bread things called pancakes is wafting through the air. I smile a little and plop down in a seat.

"Morning." Cole says to me, glancing up from his breakfast.

"Azari!" Jasmin exclaims cheerfully from the kitchen doorway. "You're awake! Here, I'll get you some food."

She disappears for a second and comes back with a plate of pancakes and a glass of juice.

"Thanks, Jasmin." I grin up at her, picking up a fork and digging in.

Mason is seated across from me and about halfway through my pancakes, he asks a question that makes me still.

"How did you heal yourself?"

"Mason!" Jasmin scolds. "She doesn't want to talk about it. Besides, it's been weeks; it's not even relevant anymore."

He shrugs, taking a bite. "Just wondering. I wish I could do something like that, that's all."

I give him a soft smile. "It's kind of like magic." I tell him, giving everyone an answer they've been seeking from me for days. "I have powers, I guess you could call them. Mine are fire."

Mason's eyes doubles in size. "Really? That's so cool! Could you show us?"

My smile dips a little. "Maybe some other time. I don't want to put any-thing here to flames."

"Then I'll take you to the field!" He suggests excitedly.

"The field?"

He nods. "It's where the pack plays games and stuff. Although it's mostly used for school."

"School?"

The little boy gapes at me. "You don't know what school is?"

I shrug, "I heard you guys mention it once or twice. I'm not sure exactly what you mean when you do, though."

"It's where you go to learn things, like math and reading and science and stuff. Our school is pack exclusive, though, so we also have training sessions as part of our school day."

"Maybe we should get her enrolled." Cole says to Jasmin in a quiet voice.

Jasmin glances at me. "Is that something you'd like? We could also put Jupiter in Kindergarten."

"Will I make friends there?" My brother asks enthusiastically. I jump a little, forgetting he was there this whole time; he's been so quiet!

Mason nods, just as enthusiastic as Jupiter. "Yeah, you'll make lots! And you'll get to play games with them and learn things. You'll like it!"

Jupiter turns his head to me, smiling brightly. "Can I, Ry, can I?"

I glance at Jasmin skeptically. "I don't know, bud. I don't like that that I won't be able to know where you are."

"He'll be fine," Jasmin assures me, "You both will."

I look down at my empty plate, stirring the left over syrup with my fork. "I don't know. . ."

Jasmin reaches over and grabs my hand, stopping my syrup stirring. "Bryce will be there," I caught a sparkle in her eye at that. "And Kiara. And you'll meet new friends in the pack as well! Personally, I think you should give it a try. It'll be good for you."

I sigh, deep in thought. After a few moments, I slowly nod my head. "Okay," I breathed. "I'll try it." Jasmin, Mason, and Jupiter beamed at me.

And it was settled: I will be starting school next week.

Chapter Twelve

I grip my new backpack straps tightly in my hands as I watch Jupiter run off with Mason into the school building.

Since the school is just for the pack, it's one building with a classroom or two for each grade. Jasmin explained that to me last week when we were shopping for school supplies.

Update: I do not like shopping that much.

It seriously drained me and just made me feel down the rest of the day. Why can't the wolves live simple, like we did in The Caves?

"Hey, Azari!" A deep voice exclaims as an arm swings around my shoulders. I immediately tense up, but soon relax as the warmth from Bryce's closeness sinks in.

"Hi." I reply quietly.

He settles down and a frown crosses his face. "You okay?" I shrug and he moves to block my view of the building with his body. He puts his hands gently on my shoulders. "Hey, it'll be fine, okay? I'll be with you the whole time."

I nod and take a deep breath. Bryce offers his hand and I gratefully take it. He gives me a small squeeze and then leads me into the school.

I honestly wasn't expecting what I see.

They all made school sound so exciting and wild and crazy. The reality was just long corridors lined with doors and milling with students. Many of which pause to sniff the air and shoot me weird looks. I do my best to ignore them.

"Azari!" An excited squeal comes from down the hall. And then Kiara is in front of me, her blue eyes bright and a huge smile on her face. "I'm so glad you're here! Are you ready for your first day?"

I give her a small shrug and inch closer to Bryce, the stares were starting to bother me. "I mean. . . I-I guess?"

She clasps her hands together excitedly. "Great! C'mon, I'll show you the classroom!" She grabs my hand and yanks me away from her brother, dragging me through the mass of people.

"Wait, but-" I start to protest, but she pays me no attention. I sigh, so much for staying with Bryce.

A few minutes and a flight of stairs later, Kiara finally comes to a stop in the doorway of a room. Peeking in, I notice there are much less people in there than out in the hall.

The room is set up with fifteen tables all facing the wall where the door is. A big desk is in the other front corner and a big white board stretched across the length of the wall. The back wall is lined with windows and the side of the room has one big bookshelf. Posters hang on the walls, telling me stuff I don't understand.

Kiara brings me to a table and plops down, gesturing for me to do the same. I hesitantly do so, putting my bag on the floor.

Several minutes go by of students slowly filling in the empty seats and lots and lots of eyes staring at me as they go past. I've now moved to staring at the lines in the wood of my table, counting the minutes that tick by. Five. Six. Seven.

When I get to eleven, a man with a flat black bag walks in and welcomes everyone with a cheery voice that makes me cringe.

"Hello everyone! As you all know, today is Monday, Pack History Day!"

The whole class groans and I am one of them. Great, so now I have to sit here and listen to him talk about the history of their pack. I sigh, this was going to be a long day.

A loud ringing sound erupts through the room and I jump. Kiara giggles.

"Relax, it's just the bell!"

"The bell? For what?"

"To signal the end of the lecture. Now we get to have lunch and then we head to the field!"

I stand up and grab my things — not that I used any of it anyway. I mostly just zoned out for the three hours of history. Three hours of stuff I didn't really understand! No thank you.

With Bryce at my side and Kiara in the lead, we leave the classroom and head down the corridor until we reach a room triple the size of the classroom. Long tables are set up with connected benches. A line has formed to the side up against the wall, but I wasn't able to see what the line was for. I'm soon to find out though, as Kiara pulls us to the end of it.

"This is where we get food. Then we'll eat one of those tables before heading outside to the field." Bryce explains.

I nod to show that I heard him. "What do we do on the field?"

"Usually we play Cricket or Soccer or something."

I'd played Cricket, but I didn't like it very much. In the Caves, we usually played games that included our powers like Electric Tag, which was my personal favorite.

"Okay." I say, responding to Bryce's answer.

The line for food is moving fairly quickly and soon, we have our food and have found a place to sit.

I only eat a small portion of what I grabbed, I think I'm just anxious about the field. I also keep glancing behind me and around the room. I get the feeling someone is watching me and I don't like it.

Bryce squeezes my hand, "You okay?"

I nod, not meeting his eyes. "Yeah, I'm fine."

I flash of blue out in the hallway catches my attention and I freeze, focusing on the food court entrance.

I stare for several moments before I see it again, this time it's clearer. It looks like... hair? I swear it's a swish of blue hair, but none of the wolves here have brightly colored hair, and if they did, I doubt it's natural like a Dragon's is.

Like a Dragon's is.

"I'll be right back." I tell my friends, hopping up and rushing towards the door. I don't hear their response.

I enter the hallway, peering in the direction the flash of blue disappeared to.

"Hello?" I whisper-called. I was answered with silence.

And then she was standing at the end of the hallway, dressed in a brown and blue leather outfit, her long blue hair loose down her back.

"Aislee?" But when I blinked, she was gone.

Chapter Thirteen

A hand grabs mine and I jump out of my skin.

"Sorry!" Bryce exclaims from behind me. "Are you alright?"

I take a deep breath and nod, turning around to face him. "Yeah, I think so. I just thought I saw. . . Never mind it was probably just my imagination."

Bryce exchanges a look with his sister. "If you're sure. . ."

I give him a small smile. "I'm fine. Are we ready to go to the field?"

Kiara claps her hands excitedly and we head outside to the back of the school building. I notice most of the school is also heading out there.

A man stands at the front of the crowd — Bryce calls him the Coach — waving his arms and trying to get everyone to quiet down. He announces we'll be playing Soccer, something I've never played before.

I scoot closer to Bryce on instinct and he wraps an arm around my shoulders. "You'll be fine." He tells me, but I'm not sure I believe him.

There are a lot of people out here, so the first game I'm able to sit out and watch, trying to learn the rules. Both Bryce and Kiara are in, though, so I also try to cheer them on. Except I don't do a great job of it; it's hard to follow them the whole time!

For the second game, however, the coach calls me in and puts me in front of the net.

"Just don't let the ball into the net, okay? That's all you have to do."

I nod, feeling like I'm in a trance. My mind keeps fluttering to Aislee and the fact that I saw her. Even if it was just my imagination.

What's really tripping me up, though, is the fact that I saw her today in a way I don't remember ever seeing her when I lived in the Caves. I don't remember her having that leather outfit, or her hair that long and curly, or her being that tall. The point is, she didn't look how I last saw her. She looked older and more like she would now if she was alive.

Unless she never died.

But then, wouldn't she have searched the woods for me all those years? If she was alive, wouldn't I be home now?

Smack!

My thoughts are knocked out of my head as I'm hit to the ground. Blinking my eyes I realize the sky is spinning. Or I am spinning. I'm not really sure at this point.

"Azari!" Bryce calls from across the field. Or, I thought he was across the field. When I turn my head, he's right next to me. "Are you okay?"

He grabs my hand and helps me into a sitting position. He cups my cheeks in his hands and scans my face with his eyes. "Can you hear me?"

I nod slowly. "I-I'm fine."

"Alpha, she's fine. She's not bleeding and she's conscious." The Coach says from behind Bryce.

Bryce sighs and reluctantly lets go of me. "Be careful, okay?" He says before walking off.

"Pay attention to the game, girl!" The Coach tells me. "It'll save you from getting hit with the ball next time."

I merely nod and help myself to my feet. Yikes. I cringe. That was embarrassing.

He looked like he was going to kiss us! Kenna swoons.

I growl at her. Shut up, he was not! He was just checking if I was okay, that's all.

I bet he would've kissed us if no one else was around!

Be quiet! I snap and shut her out. Gosh, she can be so annoying sometimes!

When the Coach blows his whistle, I watch the ball and pay attention this time. When the ball comes hurtling towards me, I'm ready, knocking it away with my hands. Half the crowd cheers and I smile a little. Okay, that was kind of fun, I guess.

The next time it happens I catch sight of a girl kicking the ball towards my net. She doesn't look happy I blocked it last time.

The girl kicks the round white ball and it soars towards me. I brace myself with my hands out in front of me when I hear a voice from my childhood. A voice that could bring me to tears right here.

"Azari!"

Aislee? I think, and my focus drops.

A collective gasp erupts from the crowd and I blink rapidly until I can see what's in front of me. But what I see makes me jump back, horrified.

Oh no, what have I done?

At my feet sits the Soccer ball. And it's on fire.

Chapter Fourteen

- -

I don't think, I just run. I run as far and fast as my legs can carry me.

"Azari!" I hear Bryce calling from the bleachers. Kiara's voice joins his.

"Azari, stop! Come back!"

I pay no attention. Except when I hear someone completely new say: "Is that fire?"

And then: "Is she creating it?!"

Tears blur my eyes, but when I glance at the ground, I can see the fire is still spreading with my feet.

Ah crap. Kenna! Help!

I'm on it! My dragon replies. When I glance down again, the fire's out. Thank goodness.

I stumble slightly and decide to focus back on my running. I'm not really sure why I'm running, but if I stop now and go back, the interrogation will just be worse. So I head towards the woods. My comfort; my home.

Bryce alert! Kenna says suddenly. I'm only a few meters short of the tree line.

Ugh! I think. He can't follow us in! Kenna, make sure this isn't spreadable; I don't want the whole forest on fire.

I slide to a stop and whirl around. And there he is, running after me, calling for me to stop. Kiara is only a little bit behind him.

I thrust my hands out in front of me and call upon the fire from inside me. When I release it, a wall of fire stands between me and my friends. Brushing off a tear, I turn and push my way into the forest, not looking back.

I run for another good five or ten minutes before I physically can't any longer. I collapse at the base of a giant oak tree, out of breath, out of energy, and even out of tears.

Kenna, I want to shift.

Yes! My dragon squeals excitedly.

I smile and sit up, not caring I'm covered in dirt. I'm ready. I tell her. I feel the transformation starting and stand all the way up.

I watch my hands, feet, legs and arms become scaly, and claws sprout from my fingertips. I feel a tail grow from behind me and wings erupt from my sides. When it's time for me to grow, become a full dragon, I fight it off, willing myself to stay little; if I'm big, they'll find me easier.

My tremors still and I'm on four legs. Sticking out my tongue, I see it's split and snake like. When I breathe out, a small flame appears in front of me. I grin in a dragon-like way. I've shifted.

I turn in small circles, enjoying the form I haven't been in for months. I stretch up on two legs and examine myself.

My scales shine dark red, while my spikes and claws give me black accents. I unfold my wings and see black spines with bright red, transparent webbing.

I also realize I'm miniature. I must've used too much energy fighting the growth that I shrunk to the size of a giant lizard.

Oops. Kenna says.

No, I like it! I tell her, flapping my wings a little. Let's fly!

I stay below the tree tops, to avoid a wolf sighting me, weaving in and out of the top branches. I twirl and flip through the air, laughing and squealing as I go.

I feel free!

Spreading my wings to a gentle glide, I breath in the scents of the forest and the wind. I sigh in content. It's like I was being suffocated in my own smoke, and now I've escaped it and I'm in fresh air again.

I've probably been flying around for hours at this point, and now the sun is almost down. I decide my head is cleared enough to shift back, and that Jupiter must be missing me.

With that thought, I return to the tree I originally shifted at and land softly on the ground.

I'm about to transform back into a human when a leaf crunches behind me. My head shoots up along with my ears, my tail, and my wings.

"Would you look at that!" A voice whispers. A voice I am all too familiar with now.

Sure enough when I whip around, I'm facing my two best friends crouched in the dirt.

"Hey, little guy!" Kiara whispers, slowly stretching a hand towards me.

Bryce immediately grabs her by the wrist. "Kiara!" He snaps, "Don't you realize what that is? It's probably fire breathing and dangerous!"

Kiara rips her arm from his grip. "But it's so cute. And if it's really a dragon, wouldn't it be a lot bigger and scary lookin'?"

I let out huff, but refrain from rolling my eyes. Ugh, why are they here?

"Kiara, c'mon, we gotta keep looking for Azari. We don't have time to play with wild dragons; the sun is nearly gone!"

My friend rolls her eyes, but reluctantly stands up, following her brother off into the woods. Once they are a good ways away from me, I hear them call my name and decide to shift back. Checking no one is in sight or hearing distance, I quickly morph back into human form.

I stand up and brush loose strands of hair from my face. When I'm satisfied, I head off into the woods in a wide circle, that way it doesn't look like I'm coming from the same spot they saw the dragon. Well. . . Me! I giggle to myself.

I skirt around a thick tree and bump right into Bryce.

"Azari!" He exclaims, catching me by the arms so I don't fall.

I duck my head, "Oh, hey guys." I say quietly.

"Hey," He says, lifting my head by the chin with his fingertip. "About what happened at the Field, don't worry about it! Everything's okay."

I sigh. "I'm still sorry. I've been distracted today and I shouldn't have set the ball on fire, or stopped you from coming after me. I just needed to breathe."

Kiara wraps her arms around me in a tight hug. "We're sorry we ran after you screaming like maniacs. That probably didn't help, huh?"

I smile at her and shake my head. "Probably not. But I appreciate you guys trying to help!"

When Kiara steps back, Bryce swoops in, actually picking me up off the ground.

"Hey!" I squeal as he starts walking back towards the Pack Houses. "What's this for?" I catch Kiara grinning at us from behind her brother, and I can feel Kenna doing the same inside my head. Ugh! Stop it!

She doesn't answer me.

"Bryce!"

I feel his arms tighten his hold on me. "Shh. Just. . .let me. Please? My wolf needs it."

I'm still in his grip and lean back to look in his eyes. I tilt my head and give him a strange look, but I decide not to question it. He and his wolf must've been worried about me out in the woods. I guess I didn't think about that.

So, I decide to enjoy this as well. I adjust myself so my legs wrap around his waist and my head rests in the crook of his neck. Sparks fly where my nose touches his skin and I smile.

Okay, I can get used to this feeling.

Chapter Fifteen

I guess I fell asleep on the walk back because suddenly I'm stirring awake at the sound of someone knocking. I lift my head to see that we're in front of Jasmin's door.

After a few moments of waiting, the door swings open and little Mason sticks his head out. His eyes find Bryce's and he gasps. "You found Azari!" He opens the door all the way and waves us through.

"Azari?" A small voice asks from the living room. The sound of a child's feet thump their way towards us and I look down to see my brother wrap his arms around one of my legs and one of Bryce's.

"Hey buddy!" I say and he tilts his head up to grin at me.

"Oh, thank goodness!" Jasmin exclaims and I turn my head as she rushes across the living room to us. "Are you okay?" I nod and she gives me a warm smile. "I'm glad you're safe."

"Where's her room?" Bryce asks. "I think she's worn out."

"Of course!" Jasmin leads him through the living room and down the hallway. She opens the door and gestures to my room before leaving us alone.

Bryce gently places me on my bed and adjusts a pillow so it's under my head. When he's done, he crouches down to be eye level with me.

"Seriously, you okay?"

I meet his gorgeous green eyes and nod. "I-I think so." I pause and take a deep breath, "I really didn't mean to set the ball on fire. Or spread it as I ran."

Bryce smiles a little. "I know you didn't. But why did you run? You could've just come to me and we would've worked everything out."

Tears prick my eyes and I look to the ceiling, trying to blink them away. "I was afraid. If I hadn't gotten out of there, I would've been attacked with questions and mobbed by the whole school!" Apparently fighting the tears didn't do enough, because I let out a small sob. "A-and if I'm afraid to even tell you the truth, how c-can I face a whole school of w-wolves with the truth?"

"Hey!" Bryce says softly, climbing onto the bed and wrapping his arms around my shaking frame. "Azari, you don't have to tell them anything, okay? You don't even have to tell me anything! I'm okay with waiting until you're comfortable with everything here and you decide when you want to tell us everything."

I take a shaky breath and nod, ducking my head into his chest. "Gracias tibi." I whisper, not even bothering to remember to speak English.

He strokes my hair and I tilt back to look into his eyes. "You look like you want to say something else."

He chuckles. "I do, but I don't think it's the right moment for it. It has nothing to do with what we we're talking about."

I smile. "It's okay to change the subject, or even the mood, you know."

Bryce smiles back. "Alright fine. But most of it's my wolf pushing me to." He says making me giggle a little. He takes a deep breath. "Okay, I really want to take you out. Like on a date. And I know it's not the most ideal way to ask, or the ideal setting or whatever, but I just—"

"Bene." I whisper, cutting him off, and then I shake my head slightly to clear it. "Sorry, that means 'okay.'"

"Yeah?" I nod and he grins. "Okay perfect!" His giddiness makes me laugh and he pulls me impossibly closer to him. "Perfect." He whispers and I smile, snuggling my face into his chest.

We lay like that for a while, and he runs his fingers through my fiery hair until my eyes close and I let myself fall asleep to the sound of his breathing.

"Azari!" A high-pitched shout echoes down the hallway and into my room. "He's here!"

"Thanks, Jupiter!" Jasmin calls back, making me flinch. "Sorry." She mutters to me, pulling out a tiny cylinder from a drawer in my bathroom I've never used.

"What is that?" I ask cautiously.

Jasmin chuckles a little, "Mascara. It's for your eyelashes to make your eyes stand out."

I give her a weird look, leaning my body away from her and the mirror we are standing in front of. "Why?"

She shakes her head with a smile. "Just because. It helps bring out the natural beauty you have without overdoing it."

I narrow my eyes, "Yeah, but why? I mean I think I'm fine how I am."

"I like your confidence in yourself, Azari, but trust me on this one. You'll like it."

I relax slightly, standing straight again. "Okay. . . But you do it, I'm not so sure about this."

She giggles and gently grabs my chin and angles my head towards her. "Okay, look straight ahead and blink slowly."

I did as she told me to until suddenly there was a tiny black stick coming at my eye. I flinched out of her grip in horror.

Jasmin sighs. "It's okay, Azari, I won't poke you in the eye. Just hold still."

I groan but oblige, blinking slowly as she draws the tiny wand of paint-like substance over my eyelashes. It takes a lot for me not to flinch away; it feels so strange!

"Azari!" Jupiter calls again.

"Almost done," Jasmin tells me. "This is the last thing we need." After another minute or two, she screws the wand back into the cylinder thing and claps her hands together with a wide smile. "You're so beautiful!"

I return the smile and glance in the mirror. My mouth drops open slightly. "Woah." I whisper. "I look different, but yet the same and my brain can't figure it out!"

Jasmin laughs. "That's makeup for you!"

I lean close to the mirror to examine my eyelashes. Instead of the reddish-blonde they were before, they are now a striking black, making them look long and full. And my eyes look so vibrantly green because of them, it's crazy!

Jasmin hugs me and smiles at me through the mirror. "You're welcome!" She giggles, "I've always wanted to do this for someone, but I haven't had a daughter until now!"

I freeze slightly at her words, but then an overwhelming warmth fills me completely. She thinks of me like a daughter! I smile at the thought. If my mother is truly gone, I know I'll always have Jasmin there for me.

Chapter Sixteen

"Wow." Bryce whispers when I walk into the living room where he's sitting on the couch. "You look amazing!"

I feel my face heat up, and I duck my head for a moment to look at my outfit. I'm wearing a lacy, apricot dress that falls in loose ruffles down to my knees. And from what I remember in the mirror, my hair is curled as close to ringlets as Jasmin could get it. It was a lot tighter at the beginning, but they are definitely looser and bigger now. By the end of the date, I know my hair will be flat again.

"Thanks. Um, so do you?" My compliment comes out like a question and he laughs, making me blush even more. "Sorry, I've never done this before."

He grins and takes my hand, causing electrical shivers to travel up my arm. "It's alright, you don't have to be embarrassed."

I give a small grin back and he leads me out the door and down the driveway to the sidewalk. We turn to the right — the opposite way as everything in the pack community — and begin walking hand-in-hand towards the forest at the end of the street.

"You seem to like the forest, so I set up a little something in there. I hope that's alright." He says nervously and I smile.

"It's perfect."

We walk mostly in silence, which was awkward at first, but now it's kind of nice. He isn't pressuring me into talking and he isn't blabbering. We're just enjoying each other's company and that's all we need right now.

A little ways into the woods, he turns and I see a small clearing with a basket set in the middle of a blanket. Nothing is spread on it, but it looked cute and cozy and it brought a smile to my face.

"I know it's totally clichè, but I hope you like it."

I shrug, "I don't even know what that means; and I love this!"

He laughs and lets go of my hand as I sink down onto my knees on the edge of the blanket. He kneels down beside the basket and starts pulling random items out of it. Some of them I can't name, but I recognized bread and cheese, and I could smell the meat that was in the soup Jasmin made weeks ago. I think it's called chicken.

He creates a plate full of a little of everything and hands it to me before creating his own. When he's finished, he scoots closer and motions to the food.

"If you don't like anything, don't be afraid to tell me. You won't hurt my feelings; I know you're not used to some of the food we have here."

I smile, "Don't worry, I've been here for a while now and I think I'll like everything you brought."

I dig in, taking it slow with small bites. I don't want to stuff myself in case he somehow had more surprises. After a little bit, he clears his throat and I freeze, glancing up at him through my eyelashes.

"So, um, there's been something I've been needing to talk to you about." He starts, and I can tell he's incredibly nervous.

It's making me nervous, so I start fidgeting, "Is this going back to what I'm not telling you? Because I promise I will eventually, I just have trust issues, and I'll answer small scale questions right now if you want, and —" I stumble over my words and he grabs my hand in a gentle manner.

"Hey, relax! It's not that, I swear."

I slackened my posture and finally looked him in the eye. ". . . Okay." I can't tell where this conversation is leading, and that frightens me a little bit.

"It's actually sort of about being a wolf."

I tilt my head, "Me being a wolf? Or your pack?"

He shakes his head. "No, more like all packs and like how the Moon Goddess created us in the beginning. I'm sure you've heard of it at some point, but to start, do you believe in Soulmates?"

I'm so intrigued, yet confused, by his response, that his question takes me off guard. "W-what?"

"Soulmates. Do you think they exist?"

I widen my eyes and lean back a little, debating what to say. "I- I mean in a way, I think they can. But I believe it's more like fate got two people together and they hit it off. I don't really think that the gods or goddesses handpicked people to meet and fall in love and have a life together, you know?"

Bryce blinks at me, his eyes don't hide his surprise well enough. "That's what you really think?"

I shrug. "I guess I never really thought about it. Where I'm from, we didn't have soulmates. Instead, many teenagers fell for each other in training. They'd get together and be married once training was completed. It wasn't arranged by anyone. It was real, you know?" I know wolves call their partners Mates, but I wasn't about to tell him that. And just because the wolves I am now apart of believe, doesn't mean I have to.

He smiles at me, but his eyes give away his disappointment for a split second. "Soulmates can be real too, Az. It's not like an arranged marriage. They feel connected through their souls — that's why it's called a soulmate!" He beams at the end, looking proud of his explanation. It almost makes me want to laugh.

But I don't, my brain focused to what he called me. "Az?"

A blush creeps up onto his cheeks. "That's what I call you in my head. I wasn't sure if you'd like it so I never said it. I guess it slipped out."

I beam, a happiness I've never felt before overwhelming me. "I like it." I tell him in a soft voice.

"Really?" I nod and heat flushes my face. The blush grows when he reaches his hand out and cups my cheek.

I suddenly realize how close we actually are. My heart starts pounding and I'm trying to decide whether or not I will flinch away if he leans in.

I'm relieved, however, when he doesn't. Instead, he goes back to our conversation. "Anyway, I needed to tell you something. I want you to understand why you feel this connection with me."

"You mean the sparks?"

"That's part of it, yeah!" I'm not sure why he's so excited.

"Well, what about it? I've always felt different around you, and I didn't know why. Will you tell me why?"

Bryce chuckles and squeezes my hand. "I'm getting there." He pauses and takes a breath, "Soulmates are real, Az. Serena the Moon Goddess assigns them from birth. But it's not like an arranged marriage, it's real. It's still fate how they meet and how they get close. The only way it compares to how humans do it is the connection; the sparks, the natural feeling of wanting to be with your mate. It's all part of it."

I stared at him.

"Azari?"

I blinked and slowly nodded. "I think I'm starting to understand. But can I ask something?" He nods enthusiastically. "How do you know the connection is real and that the sparks really mean it's the right person? I mean, sparks can't be all it is right?"

He chuckles, "Of course not! The sparks are only physical contact with your mate. The rest is the feeling you get when you look at them. How your heart soars when they smile or..."

At the beginning of his little speech, I'm smiling. But then I think about what he's saying and my smile drops. I pretty much stop listening to what he's saying.

"Az?"

I look up and take a breath, almost afraid of what the answer will be. "How do you know so much about this? Do you have a soulmate?"

"Really?" He deadpans. I blink. "Azari, I know you're not stupid. I know you've somehow already figured this out on some level. Your subconscious has told you what we are to each other, you're just afraid of it."

I stare at him, bewildered. "How-how did you figure all that out?"

He shrugs, "I know you, Az. We haven't known each other very long, but I feel like I've known you my whole life."

"Me too." I whisper. "It's the mate thing, isn't it?"

He grins and nods. "You're my soulmate, Azari. And that doesn't mean you have to immediately love me or anything, don't feel pressured into this. But I want to let you know that I think I'm in love with you. I'm not asking for you to say it back, so don't freak out." He adds when I widen my eyes and lean away slightly.

"Thank you." I tell him. "For everything. For this date, for explaining things, for opening up. I appreciate it." And now the guilt hits me. He just shared so much with me. Why can't I do the same? Why can't I open up and let him in?

I never get to even try, though, because suddenly a loud and short crunch! sound makes us both jump. I turn to my left and see an arrow sticking up from the thickly woven basket of food.

My eyes dart to the surrounding woods and I see two wolves and a man. The man has a bow and a pack of arrows. The wolves make low growling sounds.

The growls aren't like the ones I've heard a few times around Bryce's pack. These ones are deep and menacing, and also brings me back to the day I lost my family. The day I was forced to run from the Caves and never look back.

These wolves came from the pack that attacked my family! The entire Dragon community in the mountains. I tell myself I'm not just jumping to conclusions. Something inside of me — and also Kenna — are telling new it's the same ones.

Bryce stands up and faces them, his body slightly shielding me from them. "Get off my territory!" His voice is scary as it echoes through the clearing. He turns back to me with one eye on the invaders and softly tells me to run and warn Jasmin.

Instead, I stand up and shake my head at him, taking him off guard.

"Az, run!"

"No. I'm sorry Bryce. You've shared so much with me, and now it's my turn to share. I just wish it didn't have to be like this."

"What? Azari!"

I face the wolves and the arrow guy, close my eyes, and I shift.

Chapter Seventeen

☐ Banner: Azari's Dragon form. Artist: ME (signed T.L; do not steal)
☐ Materials used: mechanical pencil, colored pencil, micron pens

Bryce I'm stunned. Completely speechless. Everything in my body has gone numb with shock.

Azari is a dragon.

Azari is a dragon!

This can't be real. The girl who sat in front of me only one second ago, could not possibly have transformed into that!

She lets out a roar that shakes the ground, swiping a clawed and scaly paw at the wolves in front of her. She's nearly double their size, but I can't help feeling this isn't her true, full size.

First of all, dragons aren't the size of wolves —generally, anyway. Second, I was getting a sense of Deja Vu. Azari suspiciously looks identical to the dragon Kiara and I came across after the Flaming Soccer Ball incident. Only that creature was a fraction of this size.

Realizing I've just been standing here staring like an idiot, I snap myself back to what's happening. I start to move around Azari, trying to help, or at least analyze what is happening at this point. But every time I move in either direction, she pounces across the clearing to be in front of me, never faltering in her swipes at the wolves.

After several attempts, I sigh while suppressing a smirk. While my mind is frustrated, my heart swells. She's protecting us! I don't know if it works the same way as wolves, but even in dragon form, she is aware of what I mean to her, and possibly what she means to me.

Azari hisses as an arrow lodges it's way into her thick, scaly armor. Instinctively, I shift and manage to work my way around her. Standing beside her, I snarl at the intruders. They make no indication they have any fear of us whatsoever.

I don't understand. I mean, they're up against an Alpha wolf and a powerful dragon. A dragon for goodness sake! Why aren't they running for the hills?

Angry now, Azari spits a flame at the man with the bow. His clothes catch fire and he instantly drops to the dirt, rolling around in a desperate attempt to put it out. Azari growls thunderously and paws at the ground, her long claws miss the guy by inches.

Suddenly I'm pushed to the ground. Focusing too much on my mate, I'd gotten distracted long enough for one of the wolves to pounce. He bites into my neck and I howl in agony. Writhing violently, I manage to flip him off me and leap to my paws. This time I'm ready.

When he pounces, I rise to meet him, slashing away at his dirt brown pelt. We both snap in each other's faces, trying to latch onto the opponent's vulnerable neck. I swipe at his underbelly, narrowly missing when the ground slightly shakes from another dragon growl. My opponent takes this opportunity and claws at my face. He catches my nose and I recoil, the skin on my muzzle stinging like crazy. Angered, I lunge at him, knocking him to the ground and pinning him there. Using my hind legs, I claw furiously at the soft fur of his underbelly until he's howling in pain. He slithers from underneath me and disappears into the foliage surrounding the clearing.

A hiss of pain come from my right and I snap my head towards my mate, ready to help her in any way. An arrow sticks out from her side while the other wolf's teeth are firmly locked on her hind leg. Her spiny tail whips through the air, trying to get him off. The human stands in front of her, loading arrow after arrow. I bunch my hind legs to go after the human and let her focus on the wolf, but she suddenly takes off into the air, leveling herself with the branches of the trees. The powerful wind from her wings sends the human sprawling across the clearing, but to my surprise, the wolf hangs on tight, going into the air with her!

I growl and leap on top of the downed human. While I'm snarling in his face, he merely wipes the drool off his cheek and gives me a hard look.

"I don't know what you're doing, hanging around a dragon like this, Boy. But take my word, you don't want to be for very much longer." His voice was deep and rough, and it kind of reminded me of gravel. My growl halts in my throat, and I choke a little. What does he mean?

"They're dangerous creatures, I tell you! But I can help you get rid of them, and your pack would be a great help to me." My growl was deep in my throat, and I debate killing him on the spot. He just laughs, but it fades when a yelp comes with the thud of something hitting the ground. We both turn our head to see the wolf that had been attached to Azari was now stunned on the grass in a heap of grey fur.

While I'm distracted, the man kicks the wind out of me and shoves my paws off his shoulders, making me trip over them and bang my chin on the ground. He takes this chance and dashes away into the trees. A ball of fire follows him, splashing against the tree next to him and erupting the bark into flames. A second later, the fire vanishes.

I scramble to my paws, taking a couple bounds after the guy, but halt when I realize it's no use. Instead, I spin around to see Azari — as a human — crouching beside the wolf. With a sweep of her fingers across her thumb, she sets the body on fire before standing up and walking back to our picnic blanket, not meeting my eye.

I growl, but not menacingly. More like asking if she was okay, although I doubt she understands. I pad over and sniff her everywhere, my wolf checking if she's alright. She just stares at her lap.

I whimper and she gives a slight shake of her head, as if blocking the sound out. Hurt, I lower my head and walk away, knowing we won't get anywhere while I'm a wolf. I trot into the trees and find a pair of sweatpants tucked under the roots. I shift and tug them on as fast as I can before slowly walking back out to the blanket.

"Azari," I say softly, wanting to let her know I'm not upset. "What's wrong?"

She stays silent for a while, fidgeting with her hands. When she finally looks up, there are tears in her eyes.

"Hey!" I exclaim, still keeping my voice incredibly soft. "What's wrong? Oh, please don't cry!"

"I'm sorry." She chokes out and I'm dumbfounded. What can she possibly be sorry for? "I-I lied to you, and you've been so nice. But all I've been is secretive and strange."

Without thinking, I scoot close to her and pull her into my arms. After a stiff moment, I'm relieved when she melts into the hug and buries her face in my neck. "You have nothing to be sorry for, Az. I told you, I'm okay that you are slow to trusting me. It's okay!"

She jerks back from me and her eyes were wide and tearful. "But it's not okay!" She cries. "You were willing to share everything with me, and what do I give you in return?" She just shakes her head and looks down again.

"No," I say, "Azari, don't do this. I'm not upset, don't you see?" I wipe the tears from her cheeks and smile. "You've gone through a lot in your life, and it's okay for you to be slow with your feelings towards me. I'm prepared to earn your affection as slow as you need. But I'm here for you, and—and I love you." She draws in a sharp breath and I hug her close to me again. Her arms wrap around my neck and I can tell I took some of her worries away. But I'm afraid I might have added more as well.

But just as I am about to pull back to start going home, I hear her mumble into my chest, "I think I love you too."

Chapter Eighteen

"Wh-what?" I stutter as I pull back. This time she's smiling, and she reaches up to wipe her tears from her face.

She shrugs, "it's been playing in my mind for a little bit, but I was afraid. I didn't know if the connection was real, and I was terrified you'd find me horrifying when you realized what I was. And I was scared you would be upset that I've been hiding half of myself from you this whole time."

I grab her hand, stopping the words from tumbling so quickly out of her mouth. "Do you realize you talk a lot when your nervous?" I chuckle, "or you don't speak at all!"

She smiles sheepishly and I peck her nose, making her giggle. Suddenly, I feel like there are absolutely no secrets between us; we're free from the hiding, the shyness, and the distance. I can truly be her mate!

"It's okay to be afraid." I tell her softly, earning a small smile in return. "I was afraid too." She rolls her eyes at that. "No, really!" I insist, "meeting my mate was terrifying, I didn't know how you would feel, now you would act towards me, if you'd even want to get to know me!"

She laughs, and the sound is complete music to my ears. "And then I made it ten times worse."

"Stop saying things like that." I meet her eyes and she blinks in confusion. "You didn't make it worse, you made it an adventure. You know, if I had a regular wolf for a mate, things would be quite boring."

She giggles and shakes her head until she suddenly stiffens against me. "Wait, you were terrified to meet me?" I nod, realizing she's backtracking in our conversation. "Did you know I was here before you saw me?"

I gulp, suddenly realizing I've slipped a little. "I saw Jasmin walking you home from the Doctor's and I was curious because I didn't recognize you — and I know my entire pack."

"You were those green eyes!" She whispers hoarsely and I tilt my head. She meets my eyes again and laughs. "That was you!"

"What are you talking about?"

"The first day, when I got home —" I smile that she calls it her home — "I looked out my bedroom window. Two green eyes stared back from a couple streets over."

I give he a sheepish look. "I knew you were my mate that day. So, I begged my parents to formally meet the kids the Terry's had brought home."

"Well, I'm glad you did." She whispers and buried her head in my neck again, making my wolf purr in delight.

Capturing the moment, we stay like this for several minutes. Finally, my mind drifts to how long we've been out here. I need to warn the pack about those wolves.

"C'mon," I say, shifting so she sits up. "Let's get going."

She moves away slightly before helping herself up. Suddenly I realize she's in the same clothes as before she shifted. I give her a strange look and glance at her outfit.

She grins, "I don't shred clothing when I change."

"Lucky!" I grumble, gesturing to the sweatpants I found in the woods.

She takes a step towards the picnic basket before crying out and nearly tripping. I'm at her side instantly. "Az?"

"My foot." She whimpers a little and I remember those wolves biting at her feet. I'm worried she got seriously injured.

I sweep her up into my arms and she squeals. "Bryce, I'm fine! It's just a —" she lifts her foot towards her face to examine it. "Oh. I'm bleeding."

I glance at her worriedly and she just grins at me until I chuckle. "Stop, you're injured. We need to get you to the Pack Doctor."

Azari shrugs. "If you put me back down, I'll just heal myself."

I nearly drop her. "What?"

"Remember the day we met?"

"Yeah. What about it?"

"Aaaand I set myself on fire. Did you ever notice my snapped leg was suddenly fine?"

I gape at her in amazement. "You can heal yourself just like that?" She nods. "What the hell?! That's so unfair! Thanks a lot, Selene!" I shout at the sky. Azari throws back her head and howls with laughter.

"Alright let me down and step back." She orders when she calms down. With my wolf arguing at me to do the opposite and just run her home, it's difficult to finally set her on the grass and let go. Within seconds, fire has engulfed her completely.

The wall of flames climbs higher and higher and I notice a shadow of a wing in the midst of it all. Her dragon was actually healing her! Just before the fire spreads enough to touch a tree, it's out, the final hiss fading in the wind.

She's curled in a ball on the grass, and every muscle in my body screams to go help her. But not a second goes by before she's on her feet and beaming at me. "Alright, I'm good now."

I laugh walk over to grab her hand, leading her into the woods and towards the Pack. She glances behind us at the blanket and food.

"Wait, what about our stuff?"

I shrug and don't even turn to look. "I'll have someone come take care of it tonight."

She looks concerned, but doesn't fight me on it. We walk in silence until we can see the Tarry's house up the road. "I had a wonderful time today." She says quietly, "you know, before the wolves attacked. And after."

I grin and squeeze her hand. "Me too. And I'm glad I got to see who's behind the fire in you."

I discretely notice her peeking at me under her lashes. "Kenna," she whispers.

"Huh?"

"My dragon. Her name is Kenna."

I smile wider, "well then I'm glad I got to meet Kenna today!"

She giggles and we walk up the driveway to her front porch. She reaches for the door handle, but I spin her back around before she touches it. Not wasting a moment, I lower my lips to hers and give her a gentle kiss.

"Until next time," I whisper as I pull away, letting go of her hand and walking to my car. Before I get in, I glance back at her, waving goodbye. I chuckle when she just stands incredibly still, stunned by the kiss. I can tell she isn't unhappy with it, just surprised by it.

I pull out of the driveway and as I head down the street, I see her finally go inside. A sharp breath escapes me, and I feel almost lightheaded with happiness. But by the time I pull up to my own house, a feeling of uneasiness creeps to my bones.

Those wolves that attacked us, I have to get it the bottom of why and how they got through our borders. What if the pack was unsafe now? With a sigh, I get out of my car and walk to the front door. Just as I'm about to go inside, a flash of blue goes by in my peripheral view, disappearing into the surrounding trees.

Chapter Nineteen

I close the front door behind me and lean against it. My eyes are slightly wide and I'm shaking a little, but a huge smile is plastered on my face.

"Azari, Honey?" Jasmin calls as she gets up from the couch. "Are you alright?"

I flick my eyes towards her and nod slowly. "He kissed me!"

She squeals and rushes over to hug me. "Oh, I'm so happy for you guys! You're such a cute couple, and I bet the date was fantastic!" My smile drops shyly and she leads me over to the couch. "Tell me everything!"

I giggle at her enthusiasm. "Well it was a cute little picnic in the woods." She sighs in content, making me laugh again. "He brought a blanket and an assortment of food. It was really nice!"

She beams, "what'd you guys talk about? Wait, never mind, that's probably personal; I don't need to know."

I decide to just continue and not answer the question yet. I'm not sure if she knows about Bryce being my mate. "Well it was going great until an arrow landed on the basket." Her smile drops instantly, her expression becoming intrigued and fearful.

"Someone shot at you?" I nod and she gasps, grabbing my hand. "Who was it? We're they Wolves?"

I nod again. "It was a man and two wolves. They were definitely Weres. And then. . . they just attacked us."

Jasmin's eyes were very wide. "What did you do? Why didn't you run back here?"

I look down and fiddle with my hands, knowing I'm going to have to tell her everything or I'll be pestered for days on end. "I came clean."

She stills, thinking this through. Before she can say anything else, little footsteps run down the stairs and suddenly Jupiter is on my lap. "Hey, Buddy!"

He grins at me. "Ry, you're back!"

I giggle. "I am! I'm telling Jasmin all about my day." I kiss the top of his head, "I think it's time to tell her."

Jasmin sucks in a breath, and Cole speaks up — who I didn't even know was standing in the doorway with Mason next to him. "Are you sure?" He says, "you shouldn't feel pressured into this."

I shake my head. "I'm not. I showed Bryce today, not really by choice, but it was long overdue anyway. You have become our new family — you took us in out of pure kindness. You deserve to finally know everything."

I nudge Jupiter off my lap, "wanna show them?"

"Shift? Or powers?" He whispers, but everyone can hear him.

"Up to you, Bud." He beams and ushers Mason across the room. Mason looks at his father nervously, but shuffles across the room.

"It won't hurt," Jupiter tells him. He grabs the older boy's hand and his own begin to glow very subtly. After a few seconds, Mason sinks to the floor, his eyes droopy.

"What was that?" He slurs tiredly. "I feel half dead!"

Jupiter giggles and crouches down to grab the boy's hand again. Soon enough Mason's eyes brighten and he seems to float around the room.

"What was that?!" He squeals, making us all laugh.

"Energy." Jupiter answers simply. He spreads his palm flat and actual sparks ignite across his skin — some turn to little bolts of lightning as he extends his arm across the room. He's careful not to touch anyone or anything with them, and I'm impressed with how much control he has over his abilities at this age. "I can also move the earth." He says calmly. "But I won't, because the house might collapse."

Jasmin and Cole are staring at him in shock and Mason just looks plain amazed. I giggle and open my palm, releasing a small ball of red fire. I pass it from hand to hand, probably scaring Jasmin half to death!

"I know you've seen my powers before, and a little bit of Jupiter's. We've only been hiding what we are to stay safe."

Jasmin finally comes around and nods. "We understand. And we've actually had our suspicions and theories about what you are," she glances at her husband. "We just couldn't decide if we believed those Weres existed."

I look down again. "Go ahead and shift, Jupiter." I say, "keep yourself small."

He blinks at me, a little bit of fear in his eyes. "I don't know, Ry. I've never tried keeping myself little."

Mason holds up his hand. "Wait! You can control your size? Dude, that's awesome!"

I smile and place Jupiter on the couch. "Alright, I'll shift."

Cole and Mason walk over and sit on the couch between Jupiter and Jasmin. I take a deep breath and close my eyes, calling deep inside myself to Kenna. Soon, I feel the transition start. My arms form wings, my spine forms spikes, and my head becomes reptile-like. My skin becomes scaly and red, the accents across it turn black, and right before I'm fully changed, I stuff the growth to the back, keeping myself small. About the size of an overgrown lizard.

"I knew it." Jasmin whispers and I flick my snake-like tongue out, spinning in a circle for them to see. I flap my wings and Mason hops off the couch to come see me up close.

"Woah!" He says quietly. "You're an actual dragon!"

I flick my tongue out again and flap my wings a little, hovering a few inches for a second. When I land back on the carpet, I shift back to my human form, stumbling from the motion a little.

I look at Mason kindly, "yes. I'm an actual dragon."

"Wow!" Jasmin breathes while Cole asks, "so how come he can do the energy thing, but you can do fire?"

I fold my legs under me and sit down on the living room floor. "Where we come from, our powers aren't necessarily genetic. If that were the case, everyone would be bigeneri. Or hybrids."

"So there are different categories or something?" Jasmin asks.

I nod, "something like that. Everyone has a base element they are born with: Fire, Water, Earth, Air. However the qualities of those elements don't develop until the kid is a certain age; and it's not a set age, it's random. It's also usually when they shift for the first time."

"So you're Fire, right?" Mason's eyes are wide with admiration. "But then what is Jupiter?"

"Earth." My brother pipes up.

Cole looks as if he's trying to wrap this all around his mind. "But your powers. . ." He glances at Jupiter.

I smile and answer for him, "like I said, we all have a base element. Some elements have sub-divisions. Fire and Air do not. Water has one: Ice. Earth has three: Energy, Agriculture, Darkness."

"So if someone is Earth, they have all three?"

"Not necessarily," I explain. "Some can, yes, but many have only one; some have none. But if you are one of the subs, you also have the main element's powers. For Earth, that's quakes and terrain."

"That's what we felt when we first found you, wasn't it?" Jasmin lights up as she puts the pieces together.

Jupiter nods shyly. "I was showing Ry my control over my powers. I made the earth shake and then you guys appeared."

"What about your parents?" Jasmin asks, "I know why you left 'the Caves,' but what kind were they that led you two to become so different?"

I smile sadly as I picture my mother's bright red hair. "What I meant by it's not genetic, is that we don't get a mix of our parents. We take completely after one or completely after the other. Mother was Fire, like me."

"Your father was Earth then, right?" Cole asks, looking proud of himself for actually figuring something out with all the information I was throwing at them.

I shake my head and his pride falls, making me chuckle. "He was Water." Suddenly a series of memories with Father and Aislee flash through my mind. When they're gone, I remember how I saw her at school last week. I glance around the room, looking at all the windows. Is she here now? If she is, why doesn't she come see us?

"You alright?" Jasmin asks, climbing off the couch and across the floor to wrap me in a hug. I nod against her shoulder, unsure of what to tell her. "That was a lot for one day." She whispers, "you don't need to tell us anything else right now, maybe it's time to get some rest."

I don't really feel like I need sleep, but I don't argue. My mind is spinning as I hug everyone goodnight and stumble to my room. My heart pounds and Kenna enters my mind to warn me of something too late. I swing open my door and nearly jump out of my skin. Standing at the edge of my bed is my sister.

Chapter Twenty

"Quid agis?" Aislee hisses and I quickly but quietly shut my door. "You should not be telling Lupi what we are!"

"Nice to see you too, sis." I mutter. I'm thrilled she's here, but at the same time I'm extremely upset by her presence.

She glares at me, her ice blue eyes on fire. "What is wrong with you?" She hisses. "Do you not remember Mother's warning?"

I shrug, even though I fully remember what Mother said to me the day we left. But living here, I've come to see that it's not all bad.

She takes a few steps closer and I hold still as a statue. "What about everything Mother taught us? Are you just going to throw that all out over a boy?"

I feel my palms heat up, and I want nothing more than to chuck a flame ball at her head. She should know better than to be messing with a Fire like this.

"Well maybe," I spit back at her, "Mother was wrong!"

She takes a step back, her eyes wide. I extinguish the fire in my hands and blink. I don't think either of us were expecting that out of me.

After a moment, she recovers. "I saw you, in the clearing in woods. I saw you eat strange foods and talk to a strange Wolf before getting shot at by hostiles!"

My eyes form slits. "Well if you were just watching us, why didn't you come help us?" My voice raises slightly. "In fact, if you've been alive all this time, why didn't you come get us?! We've only been in this pack for a couple of months! Where were you for the last four years?"

She opens her mouth to answer but a knock on my bedroom door cuts her off. "Azari?" Jasmin calls and my eyes stretch wide open. Both of us freeze. "Honey, are you alright? Who are you talking to?"

"She heard us?!" Aislee hisses and I glare at her stupidity.

"Wolf hearing?" I remind her under my breath.

"All good!" I call out, hoping it's enough to send Jasmin on her way.

"Can I come in?"

I panic, my eyes darting around the room for some excuse to keep her out. "Um. . . I'd rather you don't. I'm, um, getting changed!" I shuffle around, trying to create the sound clothes would make.

"Alright, Honey, if you're sure you're fine. Just let me know if you need anything." I hear her footsteps fade and let out a breath I didn't realize I've been holding. When any noise from Jasmin is gone, I whirl back around to face my sister.

She beats me to it, "Azari, I know you're upset, but just listen to me!" I huff, but don't interrupt. "When I got trapped under that rockfall during the attack, I was knocked out for an entire week. When someone finally dig me out, everything had changed.

"Half the Caves were collapsed or destroyed. They used more than just their wolves, they used bombs and catapults! It was horrifying. When I became strong enough, I went to the woods to search for you, praying you made it. But I couldn't find you anywhere! I did try, I swear."

I keep my gaze hard as I cut in. "Four years, Aislee, four years! We never left that forest. So, I'm sorry, but I don't believe you."

She looks down, and I know that means she didn't tell me everything. "Just come home, Azari. Let yourself be a dragon once again!"

I roll my eyes, "I never stopped being a dragon, Aislee."

"You could be a free dragon." Her eyes hold a glint that makes me not so sure what she's saying is true. "Come back to where you belong. Where you were born and where you should be!"

I sigh aloud, "let me sleep on it."

She echos my sigh. "Alright, I'll leave you alone. But I'll be back in the morning."

When I blink, she's gone. I rush to the window, trying to see where she went, but it's pitch black outside, and she left no trace behind whatsoever. Confused, I rest my forehead against the glass and close my eyes.

Do I go? Or do I stay? If I left, what would happen here? What about Jasmin? And Cole and Mason? They were my new family. What about Kiara? What about Bryce?

My eyes flash open and when I lift my head, it's like the first night here all over again: green eyes pierce the night from afar, and it feels like they're looking right at me, pressuring to make a decision too. What about you? I ask them silently. If only he could hear me.

I'm groggy when I wake, and slightly disoriented. Blinking my sticky eyelids open, I nearly scream out loud when I see Aislee standing next to the bed and smiling at me.

"I missed you." She says and I groan.

"What time is it?"

"Four." Her answer is so casual it takes me a second to process her words.

"In the morning?! Aislee are you insane? I need more sleep than this!"

"No you don't, you're a dragon! That's exactly why you need to come home. You need to re-learn what it feels like to be a dragon!"

"This is not some movie about becoming one with a wild reptile, Aislee!"

"What's a movie?" She shakes her head, "never mind. Just come on! I can't wait any longer, and now is the perfect time to get out of here!"

I barely have time to think because she's pulling me out of bed and helping me into shoes. "Stay here," she says, "I'll go get Jupiter."

"Wait!" I grab her arm. "No, he won't recognize you; you'll just scare him! I'll go."

She sighs, "fine, but you need to hurry."

"Do you want us to come or not?" I snap, but before she responds, I've opened my door and am already creeping down the hall. Something clatters in the kitchen and I halt in my tracks. Who is in the kitchen at four in the morning?!

I make a fast decision and shift. As I change, I force myself smaller. Come on! I will myself to shrink farther than I've ever gone. Little more! All the way until I'm insect size. When I finish, I want to laugh. The carpet feels like a willow tree branch!

I bounce for a second on my "branch" before taking off through the air. I buzz down the hall and turn left to avoid the kitchen, going through the living room and up the stairs. I follow the path to my little brother's room, slipping through the cracked open door and silently shifting when I'm in.

"Jupiter!" I whisper as I shake his shoulders gently to wake him up. "Jupiter, bud, wake up!"

"Ughh," he groans softly and I shush him to keep him from waking Mason up, who is sleeping above him in the top bunk. "Azari?" He mumbles.

"It's me, Jupiter, come on!"

"Where are we going?" He matches my hushed tone as he crawls out from his covers.

"Home." I tell him and he looks at me with wide, confused eyes.

"But, Ry, we are home!" He giggles, "or did you forget?"

My eyes well with tears, and I have to try everything I can to keep them from spilling over. Because a little voice inside is asking me if he could be right. What am I going to lose if I go back to The Caves? But what could I gain?

I shake my head to clear the thoughts and grab my brother's hand. "We're going back to the dragon's homeland, Jupiter."

He lights up, and I smile back. "But no one knows we're leaving so we have to be sneaky, okay?"

"I can't say goodbye to Mason? And what about Jasmin and Cole?"

That hits me hard. Bryce will come over later to find me gone. Jasmin will wake up to find Jupiter and I not in our rooms. I shove the images from my mind. That isn't important right now. We are going home, where a dragon belongs!

"Just follow me, Jupiter."

Treading softly, we creep down the hallway and down the steps. At the bottom of the stairs, I unlock the front door and slowly open it, rushing a sleepy Jupiter out to the porch. Hopefully Aislee was outside waiting for us.

Sure enough, she's standing near the house in the shadows, and when we walk across the driveway, she comes out. "Ready?"

I nod, swallowing hard and forcing myself not to turn back and look at everything I'm leaving behind. I make sure especially not to look at the Alpha's house.

"Let's go home."

Chapter Twenty-One

"Who are you?" Jupiter asks Aislee, looking up from the forest ground as we walk, his hand still tightly gripping mine.

Our sister looks back from her pace in front of us and stops, turning around and crouching down to his eye level. "I'm Aislee, your sister."

His eyes stretch open. "Ry, you told me about her!"

I smile, "yes I did. She helped get you and I to safety in the attack that brought us to the woods."

"I remember the story now." He nods and we start walking again. Aislee falls in pace next to me.

"Does he know Latin?"

I nod, "that's the main way we communicated all these years. I wanted him to know it in case we ever got the okay to come back. And then as the years went on I lost my way home." I sigh and a flash of the last couple months fly through my mind. "Since coming to the Pack, we haven't used it nearly as much."

She growls lowly, "you mean because you got so comfortable to Wolves!"

"Hey!" Jupiter pipes up, "wolves aren't bad! They saved us!"

Aislee rolls her eyes. "Jupiter listen, maybe you had a good experience with a couple of wolves, but know that most will not be your friend. And most dragons do not get along with the wolves."

Jupiter side glances at me and I shake my head softly, telling him not to listen to everything she says. Thankfully, Aislee doesn't notice.

"He's shifted right?" I nod and she grins at me. "Let's fly, it will be much faster."

Aislee shifts first, and then I push Jupiter to change forms before finally following after them. We soar above the trees, as the Pack is no longer in sight, it's safe to fly in the open.

Dipping in and out with the wind, we mostly glide our way across the midnight sky, a couple hundred feet above the ground. Hours go by of endless forest zipping by below us, and several times an image of Bryce will appear in my head, making me lose balance and nearly my wing's grip on the air. I need to forget. I need things to be normal, the way they should've been if I never left; if we'd never met.

But he's my mate. I remind myself. I can't just forget that can I? The simple answer is no. It might take me months to get over him, but in the dragon world, we don't have soulmates. It's a battle between the males to win the females, as it often is for animals in the wild. So why did I end up with Bryce? Why did I get a mate but no one else does where I come from?

That's why I have to convince myself that leaving was for the better. I'm going home, where things will be normal, at least the normal that I grew up with and not the normal he grew up with.

Suddenly our date comes back to my head. And the kiss he gave me before sending me inside. I couldn't leave all that behind could I? I mean that had to mean something! What if I'm making a huge mistake?

I dip in time with my heart, nearly spinning out of control and smacking my muzzle on the topmost tree branch of a tall oak. Snorting, I flap my scaly wings and catch up with my siblings; neither of them seem to notice my fall.

The sun is well above the horizon by the time I see the cave mouths dotted in the mountain. Kenna soars towards it at first sight, and I suddenly forget all my doubts as I see home waiting for me. Aislee's dragon snorts with glee and pushes faster to catch up with me. Jupiter follows closely, although I bet he doesn't recognize it at all. His dragon might though.

Aislee leads us down to the base of the mountain. On either side of the main entrance stands a Darkness Dragon. Their shiny black scales light up almost violet in the sunrise lighting. Both spring to their feet immediately when they smell me and I don't blame them, I bet I smell like wolf. They look ready to attack until they see Aislee arrive beside me. Instantly they lower their heads and I tilt my own, but in confusion. Did Aislee have some sort of status here now?

They let us pass, and with Aislee in the lead we pad into the looming darkness of the tunnel. When the mouth and the guards are out of sight, we shift. Jupiter collapses to the stone ground the second he's in human form.

"Jupiter!" I shriek, crouching down beside him. "Are you okay? What's happening?"

"One thing I wish I could do, is give myself energy." He whispers just before his eyes close and he goes limp in front of me.

"It was a long flight for the little guy," Aislee says as I scoop him up. I cradle him in my arms as we walk down the tunnel lit by a Fire's flame torches.

"Are our quarters still here?"

Aislee nods, turning down a path I don't remember being here. After a short time, the path leads to stairs carved out in the stone, climbing up.

"Is this new?"

"Yes, after the attack we had to change most of the design of the Caves. Some of it is simply gone forever."

I brush my shoulder against the stone wall as we walk. It feels familiar, but very foreign as well. I find myself already missing the wooden, painted walls of Jasmin's house.

By the time Aislee stops at a closed door, my feet are aching, and so is my back. I'm exhausted from the night we had and my heart misses what had become home. I thought I'd be so relieved to be back in the Caves but part of me just wants to go back to the Pack.

When Aislee opens the door, I know immediately that something is off. Walking inside, I know what it is. "This isn't our room."

I turn to ask where I am, but Aislee has already closed the door and is nowhere to be seen. I stare at the door completely dumbfounded. Something strange is going on, and I don't like it one bit.

Chapter Twenty-Two

I gently lay my brother down on the stone floor before rushing to the door with a yell. "Aislee! Aislee where'd you go?" I sigh with my fists against the door. "Irrumabo." I curse under my breath.

This was not the sister I remember. At times, yes, the best friend I grew up with came to the surface, but something definitely happened here that changed her. And not for the better.

I get it. The caves collapsed on top of her and should have killed her, yet she survived. It was traumatizing for everyone! But for her to become a different person because of it? I don't understand!

With another huff, I dip my shoulder to the door and lean my back against it, sliding to the stone floor beneath me. I take the time to survey where she put us. The room is dim, lit by a singular torch in the far corner, and the Fire definitely isn't a strong, experienced one. One bed is placed in the center, it's head against the wall. A small set of drawers is the only other furniture the room possesses.

I groan, feeling very much like she stuck us in some sort of prison. And what was up with the guards at the entrance? Bowing at her? What does that mean? How much truly changed since I've been here? I push myself off the floor and stumble to the bed. While I want nothing more than to investigate what's really going on, I know that after a long journey like that, I need rest. And I need strength for whatever comes later; I have a feeling it won't be pretty.

I wake to a jarring knock at the door. Turning over and sitting up, I find my brother already awake, sitting on the stone floor and playing with the sparks that shoot from his fingertips.

"Jupiter!" I hiss, making him look up at me and the electricity vanish. I stand up just as whoever is on the other side of the door gets it unlocked. It's a woman, probably several years older than me. She has grey hair — telling me she's a Wind — and her skin is that of a native. In her arms, she carries a large tray holding a couple of clay bowls. With her comes the smell of porridge, instinctively making my stomach grumble.

I push the thought of breakfast out of my mind and dart past her and close the door before she has even said a single word. Shocked, she whirls around to follow my movement, and the bowls spin off the tray. A moment before they touch the stone, they're floating back to their place. I glance at the woman, but her sole focus is on the bowls, confirming my guess at her being a Wind: she has telekinesis.

Finally she meets my eyes, "quid quod?" Her voice is smooth, and sounds much older than what I imagine she actually is.

I hold up my hand. "I need answers." She raises an eyebrow.

"Me paenitet?"

I lean against the door to prevent her from leaving, and prevent anyone else from coming in. "Our sister shows up and offers to bring us home, but when we arrive, she throws us in a room that doesn't belong to us and locks the door from the other side! I need to know what has happened here." I soften my voice at the end, praying she knows English. Most of the dragons learn it, but not all.

The silence in the room stretches where I almost can't take it any longer, but finally she lets out a sigh. She walks over to Jupiter — who has been silent and wide-eyed the entire time — and places the tray on the floor in front of him. I watch her closely as she hands him one of the bowls and a clay spoon. She makes sure he starts eating before focusing back on me.

"Alright," she begins. Her accent is thick, but at least she knew what I was saying. "Your sister is Aislee, yes?" I nod in confirmation. "Your sister is Cave Leader; she is in charge. I cannot let you out of here until she approves and gives the order. Or Tai."

"Tai?"

"Her mate. He won her in a fight two years ago and has never left her side. Except for when she went to get you."

The wheels in my head turn. Aislee is Leader. That means Father is dead. And so is Mother. I sink to the floor, my back stays against the door. "What happened? To my parents."

"They perished in the battle. I'm sorry." I nod at her words, because they are what I was expecting.

"So Aislee took over?" She nods.

"I really shouldn't be discussing this with you, but maybe you can help."

"Help?" What could she possibly want my help with?

"When I say Aislee took over, she took over. She is not ruling as your parents taught her, how she should be. She has changed so many things, I don't know where to begin. And — " she stops for a second, as if it pains her to say what else she is thinking. "My daughter, she can be pretty rebellious.

She isn't taking the way Aislee runs things very well. I'm afraid she's going to be exiled."

I stare at her. "Exiled? My sister wouldn't —"

"She already has." The woman interrupts me.

My breath catches in my throat. "She's actually forced someone out of the Caves?"

She nods, "and I'm afraid Zekaya will be too."

I let out the breath I didn't realize I've been holding. "Okay. Thanks for filling me in a little. . ."

"Zeph," she smiles, "call me Zeph."

"Okay, Zeph, do you mind if we just head out while the door is unlocked?"

She opens her mouth but I cut her off. "We won't tell it was you who let us out, I just need to go find my sister." Jupiter takes this as a cue and leaps up, having finished both his and my bowls. I don't mention it as he grabs my hand and I whisk the door open, pulling him with me out into the hallway.

The halls are damp, and lit only every few meters. I try the best I can to get us where I want to, but the battle's toll on the tunnels makes that difficult. A series of turns, stairs, and circles later, I finally hear a large amount of commotion and conversation.

Jupiter squeezes me hand and we follow the noise until we end up at a pair of wooden doors. They stand wide open to the dining hall — which I notice also looks slightly different than I remember. Several picnic table-styled sitting arrangements crowd the cavern, and at least two-thirds the seats are full.

I push Jupiter against the wall with one hand, moving to flatten myself next to him. I peek into the cave and start scanning over the dragons with my eyes, looking for specific blue waves of hair. I don't see her, until my eyes reach the back.

There, as if she's royalty, she sits at an isolated table facing the doors in peering through. She's next to a turquoise-haired man, and as far as I can tell from here, they're holding hands while they talk and eat their breakfast.

This must be Tai.

Leaving Jupiter to either follow me or stay put, whatever he chooses, I storm in there. My hands tighten into fists and my eyes narrow at my sister. The sound of my feet hitting the stone ceases all conversations until I'm the only dragon making any noise at all. Everyone shifts in their seats and all eyes turn to me.

When I reach the isolated table, I realize Jupiter had stayed back. I'm glad; if this becomes ugly I don't want to see him get hurt. When I stop in front of my sister and her mate, the first thing she says is:

"Who let you out?"

I raise an eyebrow. "You don't see a problem with that sentence?" I shake my head at her. "You're different, you've changed. And you've changed this place. What would Mother and Father think of this?"

It gets quiet for several moments. She stares at me and it's like I can see the wheels physically turning in her brain as she searches for something to say back.

"Well, Azari, I'm glad you're here." I'm shocked at this response, but I let her continue. "I have been doing some digging and searching — both before I left and since you've been here — and I have found you two perfect matches!"

A few members of the crowd applaud but based on my sister's expression, she was expecting more from them. "Excuse me?"

She stands up. "Every dragon needs a partner, sis." She winks at me before addressing everyone behind me. "To the ring!"

Chapter Twenty-Three

The crowd cheers and everyone springs from their seats. Before I can understand what's really happening, parents grab their children and everyone shoves past one another to get out of the cavern. Aislee raises her eyebrows at me and gestures for me to follow them.

Hesitantly, I follow the dragons through the tunnels until we reach outside. The blinding sunlight catches me off guard and I stumble a little. Aislee gives me a gentle shove from behind to keep going. When I don't, she grabs my arm and we push through the crowd to the front.

I gasp when I look down; if I hadn't been led by my sister, I surely would've fallen into the giant crater I am now standing on the edge of and staring at. This definitely was not here before.

The crowd fans out to surround the crater, and so everyone can see. But at first there's nothing to see. Then at some gesture from Aislee I miss, two figures slide down the sides of the bowl and shake hands in the center. The crowd cheers, but I just stand there dumbfounded.

Wait where's Jupiter? The thought crosses my mind and I start to panic. I have no idea if he followed us out here. I start skimming through the crowd, looking for his spiked-up blonde hair. My heartbeat increases when I can't spot him.

"He's safe." Aislee assures me, seeing the panic in my eyes.

I reel on her, "what did you do with him?"

She rolls her eyes. "He's fine, Azari, calm down. He's being watched by an elder dragon with the other younger kids."

I just growl and turn back around. Suddenly I'm being lifted into the air by a force I cannot determine. Everyone's eyes are on me, making it extremely difficult to pinpoint the Wind that's using their telekinesis.

"The two Fire's standing before us today go by the names Cirtron—" the crowd cheers as the muscular dragon with carrot-orange hair raises his hand to his name. "And Kenneth!" The crowd roars again as the other guy in the crater raises his arm. This one is ever so slightly taller than Cirtron, but has a very different figure. He's sort of gangly, not quite a twig, but his muscle does not even compare to Cirtron's.

Or Bryce's. I find myself thinking. Instantly, my face reddens at the thought, but no one seems to notice. Their attention completely focused on the red head, freckled boy in the center.

When the crowd dies down, Aislee continues, her voice carrying across the pit. "These two men have made it clear to me that either would make a good match for my sister, Azari." I cringe as both dragons — as well as everyone else's — eyes drift up to my hovering form. "They stand before us, under the heat of the sun, to fight for the privilege of becoming her mate."

A startled yell escapes me and I try to fight out of the hold that Wind has on me, to no avail. The power of the mind can not be defeated by physical strength. I know that. I cannot believe Aislee is having these two men fight — possibly to the death — over me. I have a mate! Whom I have grown quite fond of in the last few weeks, and who is probably freaking out about my disappearance by now.

I try to shriek my sister's name but nothing sounded through my lips. This telekinesis thing was preventing me from speaking too! If one of these guys mates me, and Bryce finds out, he'll kill me! Actually, I take that back. He couldn't hurt me if he tried, he loves me.

He loves me. The thought rings through my mind without my consent. But he does, I know he does. I may not have quite as strong of a mutual feeling yet, but thinking back to the moments we've shared in the last couple months, I know he loves me. And that was something to fight for.

I come from my paralysis of thoughts to see the fight has already begun. The two boys' size difference makes it not as fair of a fight — or so I thought at first. After a few minutes, I realized Kenneth's thinner form made him quick. He was dodging almost every blow Cirtron handed him. While he isn't necessarily handing out his own, he's at least avoiding hits.

Fight for Bryce. Kenna tells me, and I snap myself from watching the fight in The Ring. Be brave. She whispers, and I know there's a deeper meaning to that and it takes me several long minutes for me to figure it out.

I think back to a movie I watched with Jupiter, Mason, and Jasmin once. It was about a girl with fire-orange hair and a bow. The main plot of it was saving her mother, but that's not what Kenna was talking about. I think she's referring to when the girl enters a competition for her own hand. That way, she won't get married off to anyone she doesn't like. And it essentially works.

Be Brave. Kenna says again, knowing I've got her hint.

A new kind of fire erupts from the pit of my stomach. A burning desire to fight for myself and stand up to my own sister. The only way to stop those boys, is to defeat them myself. I don't plan on killing them, just fighting enough that I win myself, and unknown to anyone else: Bryce.

The fire burns inside me until I'm pretty sure it's becoming real. Being a Fire, it doesn't hurt, it just feels like a kind of power I haven't experienced before. I feel the mind hold on me cracking, but everyone is so focused on the fight below me, I don't think they notice. Red-hot flames break the barrier at my fingertips and toes. I urge them forward, tell them to consume me, break the hold that Wind has on me. I grin as they start licking their way up my arms and legs, and I can see my hair has set ablaze too.

Finally, the flames all meet at my heart, and then I burst from the bubble, tumbling down to the crater in a ball of fire; I barely hear the crowd gasp at my sudden disturbance. Hitting the ground, I realize I've managed to land right between the two opponents. They both freeze in shock as I stand up and face Aislee, who's on the edge of the bowl and looking furious with me. The crowd gets hushed.

"Azari what are you doing?!" Even from this far away, I catch a glimmer of fear in her eyes. I don't think she knew I could get as powerful to break a mind barrier. I didn't know that I could!

I snarl at her. "I am fighting for myself! I have come to realize the Caves are not my home any longer. So I will not be taking a mate that you chose for me! Have them surrender, and I will back off, but if you don't, I will fight, and I will win!" For Bryce. Because if he were here, he'd beat these two to a pulp!

The people don't dare move after my speech. They turn to their leader for a response. Aislee's eyes still show hints of fear as she stares down at my flaming form. She knows this is a fight I will win. She knows the men she's picked have no chance. Especially not after the stunt I just pulled in front of everyone.

Cirtron, the obvious stronger of the two steps towards me and I make no hesitation to flip him to the ground, and leave awful burns across his skin behind. Kenneth widens his eyes and takes several steps away from me, and Cirtron makes slow, painful movements to return to his feet. He, too, steps away from me.

I give my sister a pointed look and she sighs, crossing her arms across her chest. "Fine! You win, Azari; you don't have to accept either of them as your mate. Maybe in a year or two, we'll come back to reconsider." She doesn't give anyone time to respond before she spins on her heel and heads back to the Caves, her mate on her heels.

Chapter Twenty-Four

I let the flames on my skin die down until they go out before I do anything. When they're gone, I realize Kenneth has made a run for it and is nowhere to be seen, and the crowd has mostly dispersed around The Ring. Turning to Cirtron, I give him a nod. "I'm sorry, for the burns. I didn't know a Fire could burn other Fires."

He shrugs, though the motion seems to pain him. "Potens es, I must say."

I duck my head, "thanks, I guess."

"Don't be so modest," he chuckles lightly, but his accent is heavy. Sometimes I forget most of the dragons prefer Latin over English. "May I ask why you decided to fight for your own hand? Do you really not want us to be your mate, or are you just trying to spite your sister?"

I sigh. "Both. She needs to know not everything is about her. But I also kind of already have a mate."

"Oh! I hadn't known. Well, congratulations, Azari, est felix guido." I barely have time to tell him thank you before he's limping away. I watch him shift into his bright orange and red dragon when he reaches the edge of the bowl. Using his wings — slightly injured from the fight — and claws, he scrambles up over the rim and disappears from view.

Alone now, I stretch my hands out in front of me. It's going to be hard getting over the fact that I just did that. I stood up for myself, and I broke from a mind hold, something I've never heard possible! I stare at my fingertips, I really am a powerful one, aren't I?

The next couple days go by, and it's strange. The dragons that pass me in the hall duck their heads as they scurry away. It's almost as if they're fearful of me now.

I can live with that.

As for what I'm actually doing every day, is pretty much nothing. I take care of Jupiter, when he's with me — which is almost never. Often, he's with the other kids his age. I leave my room to eat, to check on my brother, and if Aislee calls for me. I feel like a caged animal the rest of the time.

Nothing exciting happens until the fifth sunrise after the fight. We're in the dining area, and I'm situated at the front on the left of Aislee. Tai sits on her right. The rest of the weyr are eating their dinner and mingling amongst each other at tables stretching the lengths of the room. As am I.

Mid-way through my bite of lamb, a more unsettling commotion erupts from the middle of Table C. I snap my head to the left when someone bangs their fist on the surface.

"No!" A dragon shouts, but it's a voice I don't think I've met. "Please don't!"

Aislee stands with a growl, "don't what?" An Earth scurries from Table C, up and around the leading table, stopping at Aislee's right. The girl whispers something I can't make out fully into my sister's ear.

"What, now you're going to tattle on us?" A different voice pipes up. This time I can pinpoint it, matching it to a Water. He glances at the dragons near him, their fear evident.

By this time, the Earth is retreating and Aislee looks as if she's about to bury someone six feet under. I watch her with wide eyes as she screeches her chair back, gaining the attention of the rest of the room. "Thank you, Fern," she grumbled out, "for making me aware that we have traitors among us!"

The dining hall collectively gasps, but I think most of them are just afraid of Aislee and what she'll do if they don't agree with her.

"I won't repeat what they have said, but it was against me, and my leadership. Which might I remind you is hereditary and I have every right to be in charge here!"

I swallow, unsure how this is going to end. Aislee is showing more of her true self to me every day, and this right here adds to it. I'm not sure what happened, but she's not the sister I grew up with anymore.

"Ripley, Zekaya, Audra, and Emberly please stand up." A group from Table C rises cautiously, the dragons around us staring hard at them.

"Aislee!" I hiss, "nolite nocere eis!"

She doesn't hear me, or she pretends not to. "The four dragons in front of us shall be exiled at once! They have no place here and if any of them sets foot in this territory again, I will not hesitate to end their lives."

The four dragons glance at each other in fear as they step away from the table, dragging their feet as they make their way to the door.

"Nihil!" Someone shouts. "Quaeso, ne expelleret!" It takes me a second to realize it's the woman who brought us breakfast the first day here. "Zekaya!" She calls and the Earth in the group turns around.

"Mater!" She calls back. "Non! Vos mos adepto occidit ipsum!"

"Too late," Aislee says and raises her hand, gesturing to the Earth's at the door. "You, get the traitors out of here! And you, take care of Zeph for me."

"No!" I whisper under my breath, too scared for my own life to speak up. Zeph was going to die today, all because she spoke up for her daughter's exile. This confirms my fear: Aislee is not the leader she was taught to be. She is ruthless and cruel, and if Mother and Father were here, they would not be happy.

The next few meals in the dining area are quiet, no one wanting to talk in fear of getting the same fate as that group of kids. I scoop a spoonful of mashed vegetables into my mouth and peek at my sister under my lashes. She's not looking at me, thank heavens, but instead seems to be deep in thought, heavily concentrated as she eats her meal. I don't even want to begin to guess what scheme she's dreaming up.

A day or two ago, I stood on a ledge and stared at the world in front of me. Mostly it consisted of rocky terrain spotted with dry brush, but beyond that was the forest that stretched for miles and miles. The moon shone high above — full and in all its glory — creating beams of silvery light cascading into the leaves and giving the stone ground a blue color.

At first, I just soaked in the beauty of it, but then I remembered stories from when I was a child of wolves who turned under the moon. I was taught we were better, almost more entitled I suppose, than the dogs all because we could control our shift. I used to agree with the tales, running around the room as my parents told them, feeling as powerful as the stories claimed.

But as I stood there on that cliff, sheltered away behind the boulders, I had let my mind wander to Bryce and the pack. After getting to know them and how they lived, I realized the majority of those stories were false. I doubted the moon even had anything to do with their wolves. But even still, I was grateful for them only for the fact they brought my mind to think of him. And the longer I stared at the trees, the more the ache in my heart grew. What was he doing now? Was he worried? Was he looking for me?

As I sit here sneaking peeks at Aislee, I know the longer I'm here the worse I'm going to feel. This isn't my home anymore, and coming back was a huge mistake.

Chapter Twenty-Five

The next few days, my thoughts are consumed with getting out of here. I think about just leaving without a word and flying back to the Pack, to Bryce. But every time I subtly try to make my way out, someone stops me. Whether that's on purpose or purely coincidental, I have no clue.

Besides, I reason with myself, if I were to go back, Aislee knows exactly where to get me, and I can be assured her methods would be a lot less peaceful the second time around.

Ultimately, I'm trapped here. And it seems the only way anything can change is if my sister is stopped.

So, for the next week or so, I tuck myself away, completely emerging myself into planning mode. Mostly, I pace around my cavern, but sometimes I end up on my bed and lie completely still in deep thought. A day and a half goes by before I'm interrupted — not that I had much by then anyway, but still it dampened my motivation a little.

"I had an idea," my sister announces as she burst through my door without an invite. I sit up from my spot on my bed and raise my eyebrows. "After that little stunt you pulled during the ritual last week, I realized you have a lot of power. Both for your age and the fact you've been absent from this life for so long."

I already don't think I like where she was going with this.

"What if you learned to control that power, maybe even bring some more of it to the surface?" As she talks, she saunters around the room and I'm coming to the conclusion I won't have a choice in whatever she proposes next. "I'll help you, of course, train your hands and your mind to shape your flames how you want."

"But you're a Water." I remind her.

She rolls her eyes, "I know that! But it doesn't mean I don't know some tricks about our powers. While every element is different, our energies come from the same place inside."

I suppose that was true, but I'm not sure I want to do this. Somewhere inside I know it has to do with more than just playing around with my abilities.

She stands there, waiting for my answer, though we both know whatever I say will still lead to these little training sessions going through anyway. Finally I shrug. Maybe I could use what she teaches me as a way out eventually. Probably not, but it can't hurt to try.

So the rest of the week included these sessions. When I'm not in my room, scheming ways to stand up to her, I'm in Aislee's room learning how to bring small clumps of flame into my hand or light up my hair until it seems to burn like embers in a pit. To be fair, that was a pretty cool trick to know.

I had known I possessed these capabilities when I was in the Pack, like when I set the ball on fire. Until Aislee told me, I wasn't truly aware that wasn't normal. Sure some dragons can use their elements in human form, but it was rare and still not like in a way I had at the fight. So Aislee is determined to bring that to attention.

In the days I spend with her, I learn to summon fire with a snap of my fingers, shape it in any way I desire as it sits in my palm. I'm taught to manipulate the element itself, bend it to my will. I can form it into a sphere and bounce it back and forth between my hands, spinning it on my finger as if it is some sort of game. Aislee becomes more and more pleased as the week goes on, and that is what scares me the most.

Suddenly I have a very disturbing thought cross my mind. What if she's using me. Would she do that? Would she deliberately bring me home, teach me these tricks, all for the sake of taking down what she believes to be evil? Would she sink that low?

I decide that yes, she very much would. And that is not okay.

It was because of this thought that I stall our next meeting. I walk down the corridor slowly and silently, but not appearing to be sneaky. I just really don't want to have her teach me anything else she can use for her own benefit. Especially because that benefit will probably destroy everything that means so much to me. I eavesdropped on her conversation with her mate the other day during a meal. She plans to draw the wolves out and get rid of them for good. A shiver travels down my spine at the thought of what that could mean for Bryce. For the Pack. For us.

As I parade down the stone hall — appearing more confident than I felt — I notice something. Families with young children about Jupiters age were enjoying time together. Some were teaching their kids to fly, or at least start the discussions on shifting. Others played games and laughed together, obviously enjoying themselves and being what families should be.

I smile to myself, flashing back to when my family was like that. Before the attack ruined everything I knew to be true.

I suddenly can see why Aislee is the way she is. In her mind, wolves took everything from her, from us. In her eyes, they're evil creatures capable of massacre, capable of destroying everything we have built here throughout generations of dragons. I suppose even I had thought that way just a couple months ago, when I was living in the woods merely trying to survive.

I was beyond frightened of Jasmin and Cole when they stumbled upon us, but I had gotten to know them, grown to be apart of their family, their community. I had met Bryce, who opened more doors than I would have imagined possible. Aislee didn't have any of that. She only knows what she lost and how she lost it.

While none of this justified her wrongs, and I know she's still only using me as an ally to destroy the wolf packs, but I see her in a new light now.

However, it did irk me that while these families were playing and learning and teaching, I also noticed the methods of it all were still structured in war-like techniques. Whether they were aware of it or not, these dragons were training for this war in everything they did. It was very unsettling.

"Oh! There you are!" Aislee exclaimed as she turns the bend and finds herself in front of me. "I've been waiting! What are you doing?"

Trying to appear nonchalant, I merely shrug, glancing through the arch another moment as a child beats it's newfound wings. The tiny things are flimsy, the webbing delicate, but it manages to lift itself off the rocks a couple inches. I remember that feeling, both with myself and with Jupiter. While only a few inches, each one was significant at that age. I can't help but smile to myself.

"Oh, just watching." I mumble in response.

She steps closer to me so she can see as well. Soon, a smile appears on her own lips, but while it's not quite sinister, it's definitely not as genuine as mine had been. "At this rate, we'll have more numbers than I'd hoped."

I can't be sure if she was talking to me or just making a note to herself, but all the same I was absolutely horrified. I know I should be discreet, but I probably look distraught, ever ounce of color drained from my face, as my eyes pierce the side of her head. She can't possibly expect to send these kids, these babies into battle against full grown wolves!

She nudges me, acting way friendlier than I'm comfortable with at the moment. "Careful," she snickers, "don't set me on fire with those eyes, I have actual targets waiting for it down the hall." She turns then and I follow, leaving the happy, unsuspecting family behind.

Chapter Twenty-Six

"Azari?" A small voice whispers in the dark. The wooden door creaks as it's pushed open and then closed again. I sit up on my bed, running a finger across both eyes to get the sleepiness out.

"Jupiter?" I mumble. And then yawn. Twice. It had been an exhausting week. Aislee had pushed me to what I believe is my maximum ability, and it got tougher and tougher each time. The rock in the pit of my stomach tells me we're close. Too close.

My brother climbs up the side of my mattress, not hesitating to sidle up next to me before shimmying down until the sheets cover his legs. I sigh, knowing tonight I'm losing some much-needed sleep.

I reach for the lantern hanging closest to my bed but the slightest touch on my arm stills me. "Don't."

I turn to him to ask why, urging my eyes to adjust to the dark so I can see him. When they do, my heart breaks for my baby brother. He stares back up at me, his blue eyes — appearing much darker in the lack of light — are brimming with tears.

Instantly I wrap an arm around him, "Jupiter! Buddy, what's wrong?"

He tucks his head into my side, muffling a small wail. "I don't wanna be here anymore!" He cries, "I wanna go back to Jas! And Mason!" He pauses to sniffle, lifting his head so he can see me again, "and Bryce."

I hug him tight, feeling every bit of what he's feeling myself. "I know, bud, I know. I do too."

He runs a finger across his nose. "Then why are we here? Bryce would let us come back. Wouldn't he?"

With a grin, I nod, "of course he would! But I don't think Aislee is letting us out any time soon."

"So it's true? She's being mean and keeping us here?"

I wonder suddenly how much he knows. Jupiter may only be five, but he isn't imperceptive. I know he pays attention as best he can, and he's so, so smart. I decide he should know the truth.

"Yes," I say softly, but the shimmer of bushes tears in his eyes stall me. "I-I-I don't know why though." How can I tell him she wants to murder his new family?

His eyes burn into mine. "I think you know. Azari why won't Aislee let us go?"

I glance at the ceiling, seeing no way out of this. "She wants our help. She wants us to destroy the wolves."

"No!" He cries, gripping my shirt in his fists. "She can't! I won't!" I admire his decisiveness about it so quickly. His loyalty is still strong to the pack.

When he calms down, he adds, "is that why anyone old enough to fly has been training?"

"Unfortunately."

"Can't we all decide to stop? Fight against Aislee instead?"

I smile a little, noting how alike he and I are. "I'm trying, but I don't know who would be on my side. Last time someone stood up to Aislee, they were banished."

He shrugs, appearing much more mature than even I feel right now. "Then we get banished, and fly back to Bryce!" His smile brings him to life, so proud of himself.

I squeeze him tight, effectively getting a giggle from him. "You're too smart, you know that?" I know what he plans couldn't work. Those banished were throwaways in Aislee's eyes. After the extensive hours of training I went through this week, she needs me too much to just throw me out the window and leave me in the dust. I think the only way was to wait for the battle to happen, and then ally with the wolves and go after Aislee. I can only hope other dragons will follow my lead.

The days training with Aislee continue, and Jupiter stays quiet. I'm beginning to think the only way to get away is to kill Aislee, but I don't think I could stomach killing someone like that, let alone my own sister — no matter the evil in her heart.

During the lessons I focus on the things she says, hoping something might slip through and alert me of her plans. At first she's careful, but by day seven, she tries to talk to me more. I mostly listen, and she doesn't suspect anything; I've always been quiet.

"I still think you should take a mate." She says suddenly while correcting the form of my fingers around the solid ball of lava floating above my palm.

I shake my head, but she ignores the motion and her eyes stay fixed on what I created.

"Azari, you're still a product of the old leadership, essentially making you an heir of sorts. If something were to happen to me, you would take over."

I hope so, I think dryly. Not that I necessarily desire to take her place, but anyone could do better than her right now.

She kept talking, mostly about me, but as the hours passed, I noticed that her target for this wasn't just wolves. It was a specific pack. I think back on all my conversations with Bryce or with Jasmine, but nothing comes to mind about a pack title. I suddenly am much more afraid she's targeting Bryce's pack. If she does, I can't help but think it's my fault.

"We're gonna get them back, you know. With abilities like these," she gestures to my palm, which now held a wild fire, "those Altai Peaks mutts shouldn't stand a chance."

I don't dare speak, but my concentration falters and the flames lapping the air in front of me, snap sideways. They simmer down into sparks as they hit the stone wall, landing in a small pile of ash on the floor.

Aislee watches it for a second before turning and giving me a look. With a sigh, I focus on bringing the flame back to my left hand. Using my right, I pull at the form, urging it to bend and change shapes. But it isn't budging, my mind filled with buzzing thoughts after her last sentence.

Is this all about revenge? Is her plan to take down the wolves stemming from losing our parents all those years ago? I shudder at the chill running down my back and the flames suddenly turn bright blue. I gasp and jerk my hand back, letting the fire drop to the floor. It lives for several seconds before burning itself out, no longer able to hold onto itself without my energy.

Aislee stared at the spot on the floor for several more moments after it's burned out. I stare at her and wait for her to explode. Instead, she merely whispers in a voice filled with awe.

"How did you do that?"

I cast my eyes down to the spot it had dropped to, even though the flames were gone. "I don't know."

"Azari, the flames turned to the color of my hair. It's like a splash of water hit it, but didn't put it out." Finally she meets my eyes, "do it again."

"Aislee I can't just -"

"Do it. Again."

My eyes narrow and I summon the flames — orange, like normal. I keep my eyes locked on hers, very tempted to chuck the fire at her head. That will solve all our problems!

Focusing on the blaze, I willed it to turn blue like it had before.

"C'mon. . ." Aislee urges with anticipation.

My concentration is so deep it creates a pounding headache in the middle of my head, and all the flames manage to do is burn brighter and bigger. Finally, I have to stop with a gasp. I bend over, nearly gagging from the pressure in my brain.

"Too much," I tell her, "I'm done." Not waiting for a response, I back out of her room and dart down the hall. My shoulder bumps the wall a few times as I try to get a bearing of my surroundings. Collapsing on my bed, I lean over and spew up every last bit of substance in my stomach.

Chapter Twenty-Seven

I don't go to dinner. Or breakfast. I hole myself up in my cavern and stay tucked in a ball in the center of my bed. With no desire to get up and see Aislee or really do anything else for that matter, it's very easy to stay put in one place, one position, for so long.

Until a small knock comes to my door and Jupiter lets himself in. "Azari," he whispers hoarsely. I sit up, stiff in every muscle, worried he's crying. He's not. In fact, he almost seems happy.

"What-" my voice sounds funny, "what is it?"

"Aislee isn't going after Bryce. She's going after the wolves that killed Mom and Dad." I don't tell him I figured that out already. "She announced at the meal to start getting the Thunders organized."

Of course I miss the one important piece of information Aislee shared willingly! Time to stop wallowing, I suppose. I slide off the mattress and slowly crouch down to his level.

"She isn't going after Bryce now, but that doesn't mean she won't."

He nods somberly. "I know. Maybe we can leave during the fight?"

I smile, liking his thinking. "We'll try, okay?"

His smile is toothy, the first real happiness I've seen from him in a while. But his voice remains soft, "okay."

Taking his hand, I lead him out the door and down the hallway. We don't go in the direction the dining hall is; instead, we walk towards what I know to be the closest lookout cavern. I'm not sure when the last time Jupiter has stepped outside.

"Where are we going?" He whispers, feeling the need to stay secretive.

"You'll like it, I promise."

After several winding turns and some corridors completely pitch black to the point I needed to ignite a flame to see, the surface beneath our bare feet changes from the smooth stone to rough gravel and sharper rocks. We slow our pace, picking around the pointed pebbles, our feet not quite rough enough for them.

When the caverns were originally carved, the entire surface area of the design was rough and rocky. Overtime the rocks smoothed themselves over, making the polished feel we know now. The areas leading to lookout points and exits remain rocky. I'm not sure if that's purely from lack of use, or if it doubles as a protection service, to slow intruders and enemies if they discover the entrances.

The sunlight bathes my brother's face and instantly, I feel his hand slacken in mine. His face lights up in excitement and suddenly he's not so concerned about the condition of the floor. He bounds forward, tugging me with until the rays cover us from head to toe. Both of us squint our eyes against the brightness, needing to adjust to the change.

"Why can't we go right now?" He asks me animatedly. I press my finger to my lips and jerk my hand to the side, where I know a Darkness guard is standing post around the boulder. Jupiter's eyes widen in understanding and he presses his lips together to silence himself.

So we stand there, letting the sunlight soak us to the bone as we gaze out to the forest beyond the rocky, dry bush plane.

I'm not sure how long we're there, but I know we need to be heading in soon before Aislee loses herself over my absence. I blink my eyes several times, relishing in the feeling of the sun just a little longer. It was because of this, that as I turned to tell Jupiter it's time, a small figure moves at the edges of my vision. At first I think it's the guard, but when I focus, the figure is barely more than a dot on the landscape, way out near the woods. Jupiter sees it too, and he points, a question in his expression.

I shrug, stepping farther out on the plateau, careful to stay shielded by the boulder. Calling on my dragon — feeling how exhausted she is and urging her to find the strength — I stretch my vision to the figure. Soon enough, I can tell it's not a dragon. It acts puzzled, scanning the mountain over and over before turning back toward the treeline. It doesn't take me long to recognize more figures are standing amongst the pine trunks. I don't think the guards see them, or maybe there's really not someone on post right now.

A headache slams into me from behind my eyes and I know I've pushed my dragon too far. I stumble back and Jupiter instantly attaches his hand to my arm.

"Who is it?" He breaths and I shake my head to tell him I'm not sure.

Bryce? My heart whispers, but he couldn't have found the Caves like that, I don't think I gave him enough details to. Suddenly, I regret keeping those things from him.

Even though my eyes can't stretch, we stay put, watching and waiting for the figures to come closer. As we watch, they slowly make their way across the dry, rocky terrain. Mostly they dart between the brush, but the design of the plateaus help us spot any intruders. It's wide and open and has so little coverage we can see anyone and anything.

A small group of them — most stay sheltered in the forest — make it over halfway to the ground-level entrance before a blur of black appears from the right side of my vision. It's not dark enough for the guard to utilize shadows for transportation, but they make it to the trespassers quite quickly.

From here, I can hear what the guard bellows.

"Who goes there?" The guard stays in human form, not daring to show ourselves unless necessary.

Pushing through the slight headache leftover from the last attempt, I strain my eyesight again to try and discern who it is that stand before the Darkness Dragon. When they finally focus, I gasp and squeeze my brother's hand.

"Bryce!"

Chapter Twenty-Eight

My voice had come out in barely a breath, but the figure's head snapped in my direction. I don't think he can see me from there, as I am still hiding behind the rocks to stay away from the Darkness. But maybe it's a mate thing, that he can sense me, or his wolf is hyper aware for his mate and can pick up my voice with ease. I'm still not entirely sure how it all works.

Jupiter gazes up at me, electric blue eyes brighter than they've been in weeks. "Really?" He whispers excitedly, "he came for us?"

Now that I know it's him, it's easy to recognize his dark hair, matching his sister's who stands directly behind him. Her head tilts around slowly, taking in the peaks and tumbled rocks before her.

Focusing again, I strain my ears to listen in on the conversation.

"I'm here for my mate." Bryce announces.

The Darkness scoffs a laugh. "Oh really? And you think we have a pathetic little she-wolf held hostage here somewhere?" I'm surprised the guard speaks so freely. Often we play dumb, even with wolves, pretending to be some off-the-grid village of mountain native people having no clue of the supernatural world.

Bryce squares his shoulders. "She's not a wolf."

Coming to his senses, the Darkness coughs, "your mate's not a wolf? What else would she be then?"

"A dragon!" While she's trying to stand strong next to her Alpha, Kiara's voice gives away her awestruck perspective. Bryce elbows her back a step.

The Darkness cocks his head. "I'm not sure that's possible. Dragons don't have destined mates." He must have decided to just stick with facts, knowing this Alpha isn't up for the game of dancing around words.

"This one does, and I know she was taken here, most probably against her will."

I flinch, hating that he's wrong about that. I left on my own accord, barely needing that much of a push from Aislee. But, I justify to myself, I regret it, and it didn't take me long to miss the Pack.

From some signal I missed — or maybe there wasn't one — shifted wolves start pouring from the treeline, barking and howling as they race across the rocky terrain. Bryce glanced over his shoulder, seeming just as startled as I was. He didn't give this order.

"Wolves!" A shriek rings out through the air, echoing off the smooth boulders. Instantly, the Caves becomes a panic zone.

I don't leave the lookout yet, just pull Jupiter against me as I slam my back against the boulder we're behind in an effort to stay hidden.

From the angle I'm at, I can't watch Bryce any longer, but I can see another Cave mouth, and Aislee appears from the hole. She mutters something before letting out a war screech. "Wolves! Dragons, attack!" She leaps off the cliff edge and shifts midair, her blue scales shimmering like river ripples in the cascading sun rays.

"Oh no." I mumble to myself.

Several more screeches bounce off the surrounding stones and rocks. Aislee disappears from my sight but it's not long before an Earth leaps after her, then two Waters and an Agriculture. After a pause, five Darkness guards fly off after them.

"What do we do?" Jupiter asks. I tear my eyes from the other mouth to stare at him, because I don't know what to say. I don't know how to answer that. I have no plan, no clue what to do.

"Should we hide?" He continues after my silence stretches for several moments. "Or help?"

No way am I letting Jupiter anywhere near the fighting. But I can't send him back to that prison of a room either. My eyes drag from him to the forest. "There." I tell him, meeting his eyes again. "I want you to shift and fly over to the trees. Stay up in one and keep yourself as small as possible. I will come get you when it's all over."

His eyes welled. "But what if you don't?"

"Shh, no. Don't say that. I want you safe, and I will come get you. Okay?" He nods. "I can take care of myself, and I'll have Bryce."

He nods again, wiping at his nose. "Is Jasmin here? Or Cole? Or Mason?"

"I can't say for sure, but Mason is definitely much too young. Wolves don't shift as early as we do. But when this is over, and I come get you, we'll go find Jasmin and Cole okay?"

He grins. "Okay." Throwing his arms around my waist, he squeezes me in a tight hug and rests his head on my stomach. I place my hands on his back and squeeze back.

"Bebe erit." I whisper to him. He hangs on to me a moment longer, and soon I feel power coursing through my veins, a surge of energy hitting me as if I were suddenly holding the sun in my palm. I smile to myself, he'd given me strength. "Save some for yourself." I whisper.

He steps back, gives me a half-smile, and transforms into his golden and brown scaled dragon. Flitting his wings, he hops across a few stones before hurtling himself into the air in the opposite direction all the other dragons went, where I can hear the screeches and howls drifting up here. I stay pressed against the boulder until I see Jupiter form be engulfed by the leaves of the forest branches. Please be safe there.

"Hey!" A voice suddenly calls. I snap my head to the dark cave in front of me. "What are you doing?" The speaker comes into the light and I recognize her as an Ice. Her frosty blue hair is twisted back in a series of complicated braids.

"Nothing." I pipe back, hoping she doesn't recognize me as Aislee's personal prisoner.

"Shouldn't you be in your bedchamber?" Damn it.

I shrug, peeking over my shoulder as a scream echoes around the plain. "Shouldn't you be fighting?" I counter to get her off my back.

She scoffs a laugh. "Aislee has enough warrior trainees to take on a pack of dumb wolves."

A growl rips from my throat before I can think through it. My limbs inch to pounce on her, a natural instinct I wasn't aware I had to defend the Pack. She raises an eyebrow an leans forward on her toes.

"So which side are you on, then?"

I open my mouth and close it several times, unable to give her an answer. Narrowing her eyes, she's on me in a flash, slamming her forearms against my throat and shoulder to prevent me from moving.

"I can freeze you here." She threatens.

"And I can melt it!"

Her eyes flash an icy white-blue as the arm pressed against my windpipe drops in temperature. My heart pounds, because while I countered her threat, I actually don't know how true of a statement it was. Would my powers save me if I were contained in a block of ice? I don't want to find out.

Grunting, I use my left foot to push myself off the boulder. The Ice's arm slips and I suck in a deep breath of much-needed oxygen. Barely giving myself time to cough on the air, I swing at her face, just clipping her in the air as she ducks. Reaching up, she gingerly daps the wound, her index finger returning covered in blood. I smirk.

Infuriated, she leaps for me. I roll against the cavern wall, wincing slightly as the rough surface scraped at my cheek. Not enough to bleed, but enough to skin a layer. She flies at me again, and this time I'm not quick enough. The blunt of her blow hits me in the stomach and I double over with a gasp, the wind knocking out of me as my body hits the floor. I scramble to my feet, kicking pebbles off the cliff edge as I move. I'm not dangerously close to ridge of the cavern mouth.

"I think it's time I take you back where Aislee wants you." She says, gesturing to my bent form as I try to stand straight despite the pressure on my rib cage.

"I think," I spit, "that I'm not going back to that prison cell!"

We fly at each other again, Fire and Ice tumbling along the gravelly surface of the mouth. Her skin is cold, but not enough to give me any sort of freezing. However, I'm able to launch fireballs at her as we grapple. I miss most of the time, but once I got her tunic and another lit her hair up. Both she was able to conquer quite quickly.

Suddenly, with a shriek, she kicks me hard enough I lose my grip on her arms and end up with nothing solid beneath me. It doesn't take me long to recognize I've fallen off the cliff. Calling to my dragon, I shift midair, not bothering to control the size. The second my wings sprout, Im pushing against the air, saving myself from the ground by several feet.

An icicle stabs me in the nose and I roar hard enough to shake a few pebbles off the rock wall ledges. I rip the ice from my scales and glance up to see a pale blue dragon slicing through the air as she zooms towards me. I push out of the way, and she changes direction instantly to follow me. Opening my mouth, I send a wall of fire her way, giving her no choice but flare her wings forward and stop. When I stop, I notice a few tinged scales and some holes in her wing webbing.

Ice melts faster than fire freezes. I reason. I need to burn her to stop her from following me further.

With that in mind, I do my best to dodge all her ice blasts and icicle weapons thrown at me and every change I get, I'm on offense, throwing fire and even a few spurts if lava. Lava variations aren't my favorite power to use; it takes too much energy that I'm usually drained and can't continue the spar. This, however, was a real fight and I had to melt that icy shell of hers.

Finally, I lure her closer to me by using less energy. When her outstretched claws grasp onto my wings, I falter and we plummet towards the ground, where the rest of the battle is taking place.

C'mon! I urge myself until my entire body bursts into flames, licking and climbing over every last scale until they reach the Ice's paws. Her dragon shrieks in agony as the flames crawl from my wings to her claws and up to her shoulders. She lets go and I open my wings up like a parachute to allow myself a graceful gliding hover. The flames attack the Ice and her wings begin to fail her. Slowly by surely, she floats to the ground in wails of despair as she tries to conquer them with a dowsing of water. Just as she slumps onto the rocky turf, the fire dies and she's left with burn marks across her scales. I leave her then, knowing she won't be coming after me anytime soon.

Flapping my wings, I search the slew of writhing wolves for one that could be Bryce. In this hunt, I realize two things at once. One, the majority of the wolves aren't even fighting the dragons unless attacked first, they're fighting each other.

Why were the wolves tumbling around and fighting other wolves? I know Bryce's pack wouldn't just go at each other like this, so was there more than one pack here? How did that happen and what does that mean for all of us?

The second thing I noticed comes when another Fire shot at an unnameable wolf. The wolf ends up fine, but a spark from the blow trails to a patch of wildflowers. A single rose burns against the others, and I know what I have to do. We as dragons were pretty fireproof, depending on the type, and it took a lot to take us down. But these wolves? They had no fire protection besides their healing rates. By themselves — especially if they're occupied fighting each other — they won't get anywhere. They need fireproof, iceproof, magic proof bodies on their side. And fast.

Chapter Twenty-Nine

With new determination, I scan the crowd of wolves more intently, ignoring everything but two black wolves. At first, I figure they're Kiera and Bryce, but after more thought, I hold back. Two packs here means two alphas here. Alphas were always black-pelted wolves. I remember learning this in history class at the pack's school.

Now, I study the two midnight wolves separately. If the fighting techniques alone didn't tell me which was Bryce, the overwhelming pull from my dragon did, directing my wingbeat towards him.

He's secluded, and doesn't seem too injured. The wolf is licking at a spot on his flank — a sign of a wounded spot — but I can't see any visible blood. When the wind from my wings rustles the tree leaves and tilts the tough grass he sits on, he springs to his paws and curls his lip. Shifting a few feet from the ground, I land with a thump and stumble, placing a hand on the ground to steady myself.

Instantly, his entire demeanor changes. As I stand and meet his eyes, his lip drops, his posture straightens, and his tail lifts in a happy wag. I notice the beginnings of a shift.

"Wait!" I hold my hand up in an effort to prevent the shift. "Stay in wolf form, I'm just here to tell you what's going on." His jowls slacken as if trying to argue with me. "And that I'm okay," I add, knowing his wolf ought to be beside himself with worry. I've lost count how long I've been gone, but long enough for the link between us to send the both of us — him especially — into a tailspin.

"I promise, I'm okay. But my sister is, is -" I can't think of the English word- "psychotici. She's basically holding me prisoner to use me for some of my abnormally enhanced abilities... against wolves."

His lips lift back into a snarl.

"I know I know. But I don't think it's about your pack. I think it's the pack that attacked us on our picnic; remember that?" His eyes shift to the side and I confirm what I'm already pretty sure about, "this is more than just your pack of wolves isn't it? These wolves are the Altai Peaks Pack, yeah? The ones that attacked in the woods? The ones that killed my parents?" A slight tinge of vengeance hits me when I say that, but I can't focus on that now. The wolves are not the enemy here right now. Aislee is.

He nods and his tail droops. So there, I was right. The extra on-slew of wolves aren't his.

"Okay. We need to get that pack on our side. But you won't survive against the dragons' magic. So I will take care of getting most of them to fight with us, not against. Our only target is Aislee, okay?" I stare him down in the eyes for this part. "If we can help it, no innocent dragon is to be injured or killed in the midst of this. And I would prefer my sister not die. She may be crazy and a sudden tyrant but she's still my sister."

I shift my stance so I can see the battlefield, praying no one is sneaking up on us while I fill him in. Everyone seems pretty occupied, but they won't switch sides and do what I hope without some encouragement. "Jupiter is hiding in the trees beyond that rise," I jab my thumb in the general direction, "I told him I would come get him when this is over, but I'm sure he'll be just as happy if Jasmin does." He nods, taking this all in. I'm not sure if I've ever said this many words to him before.

"Go find Jasmin, I'm not sure what her wolf looks like, and I'll go talk to the Altai Peaks Alpha."

Worry crosses his wolfy face and I reassure him. "It's okay, I can handle myself if he's a jerk. Go, and let's turn this around before too many are hurt or lost!"

He barks, sticking his snout forward to lick my cheek and I giggle, gently swatting him away. "Go he bounds off into the trees, away from the fight, his tail high and flying as he goes.

Shifting, I turn and launch myself back to the sky. This time it doesn't take long to find the other alpha, his black pelt the only one in a sea of grey and reds. I dive for him, peeling him off of another wolf at the same time as blocking the blow of a Fire from the air. He tumbles across the hard dirt, rolling a few times before he finds his footing. With a snarl, he pounces at me but I merely swat him back down. My full size way too much for him to conquer.

I hold him under my taloned paw until he stops struggling. When he finally relaxes, I shift back and hurry to speak before he takes advantage of my human form.

"Listen! I'm not the enemy! Neither are these wolves!"

The black wolf transforms into a man, and I suck in a breath and dart my gaze to a cloud floating in the sky. Wolves shift back naked; no thank you.

"You're a dragon, and I've been enemies with the Irtish Waters Pack for generations!"

I shake my head, "that may be, but right now, in this particular situation, we need each other. I'm on Alpha Addams side, not the dragons. I'm being held here more or less against my will. Bryce's pack needs your pack to fight the dragons. Specifically one dragon: Aislee. She's a Water, so in dragon form she's shades of blue. I'm going to take care of getting the innocent dragons on the wolf side, I need you to stop fighting the other wolves and to focus on taking down one dragon."

He snorts, "who are you to boss me around? I could kill you with one bite to the throat!"

I finally meet his eye, "and I could burn you down to ashes with a single puff of air. I don't think you want to try me." To make a point, I summon a ball of fire and dance it across my fingertips. Slowly it grows larger and larger and I'm this close to just saying "screw it" and chucking it at his arrogant head anyway.

He holds up a hand. "Okay okay, fine! I won't attack Addam's pack. But any dragon that isn't actively fighting with us will feel these teeth."

The fire hisses out and I stick my palm out. "Fair enough. Thank you for your cooperation." When he shakes my hand, I heat it up a little until he jerks away; a final warning before I shift into my scaly form and fly off.

It doesn't take long for the atmosphere of the fight to change dramatically. The wolves soon follow their alphas' leads and stop tussling with each other. Like I'd hoped, a few select dragons follow my lead and start handing out blows against their Cavemates. As the fight continues, more and more switch. It's soon left with just Aislee, her mate, and a handful of guards and warriors fighting for her.

With a screech, I lunge for her. She's larger than I am, and her scales are slippery due to her Water qualities. But, finally I'm able to grasp her shoulders with my talons. I push against her beating wings, forcing her towards the ground as best as I can manage. The flap of her wings narrowly miss smacking me in the muzzle.

Growling, she uses her hind feet to claw at my underbelly. Howling in pain, I let go and shift, hitting the ground with a thud. I can feel scattered pebbles pierce the exposed skin of my arms. I'm winded for a moment and by the time I'm able to get to my feet, Aislee has reached the ground and is also standing in her human form. She pants to catch her breath and I do the same, fighting to stay upright.

"Aislee, stop this!" I plead when I can breathe enough again. "You've turned the Caves into madness. Since you brought me back, I haven't seen a single dragon truly happy. Even yourself."

Her mouth pops as she goes to correct me but I take over before she can.

"It's true. All you've thought about is revenge over what happened five years ago. You take it out on me, on Jupiter, on the Darkness dragons, and even on the innocent. There was no reason for you to exile that group of kids. Your way of rule goes against everything Mama and Papa stood for, taught us to be. And for what? To murder a pack of wolves?"

I notice no one is in the air any longer. No one is fighting. They're all silently waiting for one of us to signal more attacks.

I gesture to everyone that had been on the wolves' side, "look at what you've done. Most of the Caves has turned its back on you. The only ones left are Darkness, and their trained to be loyal to the Cave Leader no matter the cost. Doesn't that tell you something?"

Finally, I take a deep breath and I let her speak.

"You were supposed to be on my side!" She argues, but her voice doesn't hold as much fire as I thought it would. "I brought you back because I thought you would want to avenge that dreadful night. I thought you'd be happy to be home."

"I was," I said softly. "But you are not the same sister that got me and our brother to safety that night. You only wanted me to help you fight. And you have shown me this is not my home any longer." I look to the left, finding Bryce's piercing green eyes standing out against his dark fur. "My home is with the pack now. I have found love, and a family, and a new life; and I'm okay with that. I will always be a dragon, and my origin will always be the Caves. But I don't think that's where I belong anymore."

She looks completely stricken, and I understand. I just don't want her to be rash about it. "I need you to understand, Aislee, and for you to leave me, Bryce's pack, and even the Altai Peaks pack alone. I don't want for you to have to die for those things to happen."

She finally meets my eye, and they hold tears. She doesn't want to lose me, and I don't want to lose her. But things are different now. We're not children, and our lives have gone in completely different directions. After several long, breath-holding moments, she gives me a solemn nod, agreeing to what I ask of her.

Chapter Thirty

The wolves don't instantly break their form like I was expecting when Aislee dips her head in surrender. Well, not all of them. One wolf does.

Bryce, having now shifted runs across the deserted plain, hurdling over the dry brush and small boulders to get to me. He's somehow found a pair of basketball shorts to wear, but no shirt. Honestly, I'm okay with that. Instantly, I blush at my own thoughts. Stop it, not now!

He slows as he reaches me, and by that point I'm just impressed he did that barefoot. Those pebbles are brutal! When he gets here, my hand is engulfed in his and his eyes scan me from head to toe several times over. "Are you okay?"

I nod and he gives me a look. Rolling my eyes, I lift my shirt a few inches to reveal the slashes left across my torso. "It only hurts when I twist or bend." I see Aislee wince, knowing it was from her claws. But I'm sure I left marks on her too.

She turns and whispers something to Tai, who has shifted and is standing next to her. He nods and jogs off towards the rest of the dragons and wolves, announcing for everyone to find their families and start taking care of wounds. I also can hear him apologizing to pretty much anyone he talks to.

Bryce pulls my attention back to him. "Can you heal?"

I shake my head, "my dragon is too worn out. We should help." I start to move, but he pulls me back to him. I squeak as his arms snake around me and my feet no longer touch the ground. He breathes deeply into my neck and I wrap my arms around him and hug him back. Thinking back to when I ran off into the woods during the soccer game, I know his wolf just needs to reassurance of my safety, of my presence.

His lips find mine and I let us disappear into the moment, my body becoming limp with exhaustion and relief to be back in his arms. When he pulls away, my eyes fill with tears I wasn't expecting.

"I'm sorry."

His eyebrows furrow, "for what?"

"When Aislee came to the pack, I went with her. Willingly. I, I ached to be home, to be in the Caves again and I barely even thought about what that would do to you. To us." I bury my face in my hands, "it was a huge mistake, and I realized that soon after getting here. I shouldn't have left you like that."

He peels my hands off my face and tilts my chin up. "Hey, it's okay. You longed to be home, I could see it in your eyes sometimes. They would find the mountains on the horizon, you know. And the mate thing is new to you, so don't be sorry. I'm not mad. Though, I did panic when no one could find you and anyone able in the pack has been searching since."

I wipe at my eyes, "really? I didn't know the wolves knew who I was. Besides Jasmin's family and yours of course."

He smiled, "you're the future Luna, of course they know."

My heart jumps when he says that, but I can't be afraid of the title. I'll have Bryce. And Kiera. Smiling, I kiss him again before he lets me drag him to the rest of the crowd.

I'm thrilled when I see dragons helping wolves and wolves helping dragons. Many are talking with smiles on their faces. As we walk, anyone I identify as Altai Peaks pack members, I shake their hand, ask them how they are, and express my gratitude for their help and shift in attitude against the dragons and the Irtysh Waters Pack.

Eventually, the Alpha appears and he dips his head to us both. "I'm sorry, about that day in the woods when we attacked you two. I was looking for a war between our packs — an unnecessary war — and it was stupid really."

Bryce stuck out his hand, "agree to leave each other in peace?"

"And the dragons!" I add, sticking my hand out too.

The Alpha grins, shaking both mine and Bryce's outstretched hands. "Peace, I promise."

He leaves then, heading towards the forest. His wolves follow immediately, despite their injuries. Because I was watching them go, my eyes were still on the trees when I see a woman walk out from them, a child on her hip.

"Jasmin!" I call and she lights up as she sees me. Jupiter squirms in her arms and she lets him run ahead. When he gets to us, he leaps not into my arms but into Bryce's. He laughs incredulously but embraces the child all the same.

"I knew you'd come back for us." He whispers and Bryce hugs him tighter.

"Of course."

Jupiter hugs me too, but less dramatically, saying he's glad I didn't die. Laughing, I kiss the top of his head, grateful that he stayed safe through it all.

"I can go back with Jasmin now?" He asks, letting go of me and clinging to Jasmin's leg.

I grin, "if that's okay with Jasmin."

She laughs and pats his back. "Of course you can come home, Jupiter. Mason will be so excited to see you!"

A smile stretched across my face and I grasp Bryce's hand in mine. If you had told me a year ago that I would be choosing to live with a pack of wolves over the mountain I grew up in, I would have called you insanis. But after losing my family five years ago, I know I've found my new family, my true family. With Bryce, with Kiera — who I can see talking with and helping her pack a few yards away — with Jasmin, and Cole and Mason. The Caves were no longer the home I belonged to, these people, these wolves were. And I couldn't be happier.